AMANDA MCCORMACK

The Cottage at Delinsky Cove

Want a free eBook?

Want a free book? Sign up for my mailing list and receive an exclusive North County Paranormal novella! 15K words of a cursed house, a missing teammate, and a case that should have been done by lunch.

https://mailchi.mp/59fca3585a24/vanishing

Chapter 1

"Good morning, sunshine."

James jerked awake and looked up from where he was slouched in the living room recliner at Headquarters. His second-in-command, Amelia, was standing over him, clearly trying not to laugh.

"Didn't you have me and Graham help you lug an entire hideous couch into your office just last week?" she asked as James wiped his eyes and tried to get the taste of stale hell out of his mouth. "What are you doing out here? Busy night last night?"

James groaned. "Ridiculously busy," he said, sitting up straight. "We were silent until about midnight. Then there was full-on poltergeist bullshit at City Hall. The security guard had our number, don't ask me why. But then we ended up down there playing Ghostbusters for two hours until Graham could put up some wards and I chased the energy out. The Foundation then had the audacity to ask me to send in the report ASAP so that they would have it on their desks when the right people arrived this morning."

"Did you?"

"No, because as soon as we got here, the phone rang again. South Worcester County had a report of some kind of ritual going on and when they went to investigate, the guy was open to talking. He said they were trying to bring on a new age of I don't even fucking know what. But they were based in Lunenburg. So I got to go to Lunenburg at four in the morning to check out an empty field. I got back-" He rubbed his eyes and glanced at his watch. "About thirty minutes ago, and sat down to think for a second before I got started on the report for that one. And the one I have to do for City Hall."

Without a word, Amelia went into the kitchen. She walked back a moment later with a massive mug of coffee, which she handed to him. "Do I want to know how long you're on for today?" she asked.

He took the coffee gratefully and took a long sip. After seven years of working together, they knew each other's cream and sugar preferences, so it was perfect. Almost enough to make it worth being here. "All day," he said. "And I've already heard three notifications about fresh cases."

"Great."

James rubbed his face with a hand, trying to will away the sleep that was trying to claim him again. "We're fully staffed today, so there's that at least," he said.

"Small favors."

"I actually wanted to talk to you about a couple things that are staff-related," James said, suddenly remembering the plans he'd been making when everything went to hell last night.

"Oh? What about?"

"What would you think about specializing the team a little more?"

"How do you mean?" Amelia asked, sitting down on the couch.

"Okay, we can't afford to lose any field agents, but we're already heading toward being more specialized outside of that. We've got Bradley on finance and logistics. Gabriella's basically becoming our team researcher, just minus the title. I was thinking we might be able to make things a little easier for everybody if we had them all officially take on those kinds of roles. Maybe I could even get the Foundation to put some money into it, give them raises like you and I got."

"Not as much as us, though," Amelia said, taking a sip of her own coffee. "Wouldn't want them getting any ideas."

James laughed. "No, but really," he said. "If we kind of consider where everybody's strengths lie, we can fill in gaps around them. But between the scheduling system and some more specialization, we could get in good shape."

"I don't hate it," Amelia said. "In fact, I know Madelyn's been studying for the Foundation's tech seminars. I tried to get her to sign up for the one next month, but she said she doesn't think she's ready yet."

"Oh man, having one person doing all the new tech training would be amazing," James said. "I'm awful at it and constantly calling it logistics and tossing it on Bradley's workload seems unfair."

"I'm in," Amelia said. "As long as everybody's good with it, I think it'd be a great idea."

"Great," James said. "We'll get that sorted out."

"What was the other thing you wanted to talk about?" Amelia asked.

"Hmm?" James was halfway through a sip of coffee before he remembered what he wanted to say. "Oh, yeah. You and I need to talk later. You don't need to decide now, but there is a captain vacancy coming up."

Amelia looked up at him. "Oh?" she said, eyebrows raised.

"Yeah. It's actually right over the border in Hillsborough County, New Hampshire. It's not the most active branch, but their captain of twenty years is retiring in a couple months and nobody on the team has shown the interest or skill needed to take over."

"Ah."

"Yeah. First of all, what the hell do you mean there's a choice? But also, they're searching for candidates. Would you possibly be interested?"

He didn't expect a screaming, crying "YES!" exactly, but he also didn't expect the long silence that greeted his question. Amelia looked thoughtful, but also a little nervous?

"Again, you don't need to decide right now," he said quickly. "But just consider it, okay? You'd be awesome at it and I know you want to be captain of your own team."

"I mean, yeah, at some point I do," Amelia started slowly. "Hillsborough County, you said?"

"Yeah, so it's not like you'd have to relocate," James said. "I double-checked. Ideally, you'd live in the county, but it isn't required. And we're right over the border, so they wouldn't be too concerned if you stay here."

"I'll think about it," Amelia said.

"No pressure," James said. "I just want to offer it up, you know?"

"Yeah, of course."

Why did she look so distressed by this? "It's okay," James insisted. "Seriously, take your time. I don't think their captain is going anywhere until at least April."

"Yeah, I will," Amelia said distractedly. "Um, I'll be right back."

She hurried out of the room, leaving James with the impression he'd done something wrong. But what could it have been? He knew he wasn't the most sensitive guy in the world, but Amelia had been working toward having her own branch for years. She was young, but she'd taken a ridiculous amount of training in every possible subject she could and he knew she'd signed up for four more in the next six months. They'd talked about it before and now she'd had some experience as second-in-command, so it wasn't like she was being thrown directly into it.

It was fine. Maybe she was just overwhelmed by the possibility.

James stood up and stretched, picking up his coffee. Speaking of captaincy, he had to get ready for a phone meeting with the Foundation. Bradley would be there to sit in on the second half of it with him for all the financial discussion, but the first part was all James. So he was going to need to slug back this coffee and get his brain working soon.

He opened the door to what was finally starting to feel like his office and walked inside. The couch Amelia had been teasing him about was sitting in the previously empty space along the wall just inside the door. James walked past the aggressively floral sofa, heading straight over to crack open a window and let out some of the dry heat of the room. It smelled like old books and older coffee in here, neither of which was nearly as appealing as they sounded.

He opened the window and let the cold air rush in, hitting him in the face. It was mid-December and the first snowflakes of the season were actually falling as he stood there and looked out over the suburban neighborhood where their headquarters was located.

Someone was in the driveway of the house next to them, starting their car before running back inside for something. As James watched across the yard, smoke curled out of the tailpipe and rose lazily toward the gray sky. The grass of their yard was dead by now, yellowed and crunchy, so the snowflakes drifting down disappeared as soon as they landed.

James wanted to stay here all day, letting the sharp wind come in and wake him up before whatever bullshit the Foundation wanted to discuss arrived. He could see exactly how this meeting would go. He didn't need to be psychic to know all this; he was just coming up on six months in this position.

The Foundation reps would have their things to talk about, generally ways in which they wanted him to do his job better. He'd smile and nod, telling them he'd take that into consideration. Then he'd ask for something in return and they'd very politely refuse his request. The next half of the meeting would involve figuring out the next month's spending. Bradley would say something dickish, James would try to figure out the best way to apologize while completely agreeing with what Bradley had said, and then they'd end the call. He and Bradley would shout at each other for a little while before joining the rest of the team on the three cases that had arrived for the day.

Oh, and there'd be questions about why the reports from last night hadn't arrived in time. Didn't James know they were very busy and couldn't wait on him?

God, it was like he'd lived the whole meeting already and it wasn't starting for five minutes.

The man was back out at his car and before James realized what was happening, they'd made awkward eye contact across the fifteen feet of yard between them. The man held up a gloved hand and waved. James waved back.

Did that guy have any idea what happened over here? Maybe he thought James was the owner of this home, just waking up for the day. Maybe in his mind, James was gazing out the window, thinking about the office job he was headed to shortly.

Honestly, that sounded pretty nice right about now.

Chapter 2

A few minutes later, James sat down at the computer and started it up, knowing full well it was going to chug along until seconds before he had to be on the call. As it slowly came to life, he glanced at the printout of cases for the day. It was a fairly reasonable set of tasks. Interview for a potential possession over in Sterling. That would probably end up going to Father McEnerney once they finished their initial investigation.

A cryptid sighting in the Leominster State Forest. That was just another day at work. As long as the cryptids stayed within the state forest, they rarely needed to do anything more than interview the source and monitor the area. That was one that Amelia could probably handle before they even finished the team meeting about it.

And then two odd deaths, which generally wasn't their business. James clicked into the video meeting program and glanced back down at the sheet as the program started up. Two individuals over in Ashburnham, a small town nearby where they really didn't get a lot of cases. One on the railroad through town while the other was found hanging in his home. Why was the Foundation involved in this?

James flipped the page and felt the coffee creep back up his throat at the full-color images of the corpses where they'd been found. Both photos were bloody, the bodies in pieces, yet still recognizable as human remains.

"James!"

James's head shot up and he shoved the sheets aside as McGovern, the branch liaison officer, greeted him from his small square on the screen.

Seconds later, Johansen and Gold also joined in from resource management and the financial office, respectively.

"Good morning," James said to everyone, sitting up straighter in his chair.

He knew he looked rough, but he could hope that it lent him an air of credibility. Maybe they'd think he had a ruggedness to him, something that showed he was someone to be trusted, someone who knew what he was doing. Even if he never, ever did.

The meeting began with the usual pleasantries. Then McGovern turned to James. "Did you have time to get that report in from last night?" he asked.

James shook his head, mid-sip of coffee. "No," he said after swallowing. "It's in the works now, but as soon as we got back to base, we needed to check a situation in Lunenburg."

"Oh, right, that one," McGovern said. "Alright, that makes perfect sense. Just get that in as soon as you can, will you?"

"Of course."

"Where is Lunenburg again?" Gold asked, her voice raspy in a way that told James she had that bug that was going around.

"Just north of us," James said. "South County caught it, but the actual action was supposedly taking place up here, so they passed it over to us."

"Just like they're supposed to," Johansen said approvingly, his elderly face unnervingly close to the camera.

The meeting carried on like this. McGovern would ask about something James hadn't done, James would tell him exactly why, and the other two would commentate. Every so often, a flash of disapproval would come over McGovern's face, and despite everything, James would feel sheepish. He didn't want to not be doing these things, they just weren't giving him what he needed in order to do them. Which was usually a full crew, but he wasn't sure it was worth even trying to get someone else on the team right now. The fact that they'd hired Graham was a miracle, and James knew it was only because of what had happened with their previous captain, Robin, earlier in the year.

"That's it for follow-up," McGovern said. "Once your other half arrives, we can move on to the next part."

Amelia wasn't supposed to be in this meeting, she was probably halfway through her daily workout by now. He was about to tell McGovern this when the door opened and Bradley walked in, still wearing his heavy winter coat. "Sorry I'm late," he said, voice tight. "There was something going on, traffic was backed up all the way to the exit. I ended up going around."

"There he is!" McGovern chirped as James shifted aside to make room for Bradley behind his desk. "We were just wrapping up the follow-ups for the week."

"Any word on the van detailing reimbursement request I sent in?" Bradley asked, pulling one of James's aunt's old kitchen chairs over and sitting down.

"This meeting is for follow-ups only," Gold said.

"Any follow-up on the van detailing reimbursement request I sent in?"

James shot him a look, but Bradley was taking off his coat and not looking at him. "Not yet," McGovern said cheerfully. "They're a bit backed up. I'll be in touch once that goes through."

"I paid for it out of pocket since the others were backed up too."

James hadn't known that and he hoped his surprise didn't register on his face as he turned and looked as neutrally as possible at Bradley. Making sure the desk was out of sight on his webcam, he pulled over a scrap of paper and a pen.

Why did you do that?

Bradley watched him write, then pointedly ignored him as he set down the pen for a response. Instead of waiting for more than a second, James picked the pen back up instead.

Don't spend your money

"We need to discuss upcoming financial expectations while we're on the call," Johansen said as James set the pen down. "There's been a few situations lately, so we'll need to reallocate some resources."

"What kinds of situations?" James asked.

"Nothing concerning your branch," McGovern said quickly. "No, we had a few cases fall apart in Connecticut after the entire team came down with the flu at the same time."

"Amazing how that happens," Gold said, then ducked off-screen to sneeze.

"But it means that the region wasn't effectively covered for a few days, so we need to look into how to keep areas covered during emergency situations like that."

If James remembered correctly, the last time there'd been a flu outbreak in their branch, Robin had worked triples for a week. But he had a feeling that wasn't what they were talking about.

"But how this does impact you is that the funding available might change," Gold said.

"Change how?"

Bradley's voice was low and James resisted the urge to kick him under the desk, even as he felt the same frustration.

"We're not sure yet," Johansen said. "But given the tightness of the budget in general, we'll need to work together to figure it out."

"Have we considered a bake sale?"

Now James did give him a swift kick in the leg. Bradley flinched and glared at him. "What do you need from us?" James asked McGovern before a fight could begin.

"We'll start by having you keep careful track of expenses over the next month," McGovern said. "Consider what is and isn't necessary and give us as accurate a read on your needs as possible. We'll see from there."

That was shockingly reasonable, at least for the Foundation. Before Bradley could say anything else, James nodded. "That's doable," he said. "I'd just ask that you keep in mind that we're understaffed and have already spent months cutting expenses as much as possible."

"You're not considering staff cuts, are you?" Bradley demanded.

"No, of course not," McGovern said, the first hint of frustration in his voice. "We're not looking to cut anybody or any essential programs."

"Thank you," James said. "We'll keep track and send you the results."

"We'll keep those receipts," Bradley said. "Make sure to use generic painkillers when someone falls through a floor because we don't have the resources we need already."

Yeah, this was going exactly as he expected it to. McGovern was trying to keep professional, but Johansen was turning red while Gold had ducked off-screen again.

"We'll keep track," James said again. "Is there anything else we need to address while we're here? The promotions list? Training programs?"

Arming me so I can shoot myself and get out of this conversation?

"I think that's all," McGovern said. "I assume you've heard about Hillsborough, so if there's anyone on your team considering applying for the position there, send them my way. Same with the one in North Aroostook County. That one is open immediately."

James couldn't quite tell from the camera angle, but he was pretty sure all heads turned in Bradley's direction at the same time. At the moment, James would gladly send him to the Canadian border to fight their Bigfoot.

"I'll do that," James said.

"I've got nothing to add," Johansen said.

"Same," Gold said through a stuffy nose.

"Alright, let's sign off," McGovern said. "Thanks for coming. James, just get those reports in by the end of the day if possible."

James had a feeling the meeting was supposed to go longer than this, but he wasn't about to complain. So instead, he just nodded. "I'll do that."

They hung up the call, and James immediately turned to Bradley. "Fucking really?"

"What?" Bradley demanded, looking down at the case notes on the desk. "Are you just going to let them cut our funding little by little?"

"No, but they were clearly going to discuss everything with us, not keep it some big secret. You didn't need to go in guns blazing. They're asking us to keep track of expenses, not sell off our equipment."

"For now," Bradley said. "And by the way, I always keep track of expenses. You should know that. It's literally part of my job."

He flipped the page over. "They always do this and then they- Jesus."

The gory color photos were looking up at them, cutting off whatever they had been about to fight over next. "Yeah, that's today's case," James said.

"What the hell did that, and are we going to have to fight it?"

"No idea, and no idea," James replied. "Better get those generic brand painkillers ready, huh?"

Bradley looked at him, then back down at the page. Then he ran a hand over his thin face. "I'm going to make some coffee," he said, and walked out.

James took a breath, then glanced back out the still-open window. The car was back in the driveway next door.

Chapter 3

All good intentions of showering between shifts had gone out the window between the multiple tasks and falling asleep for all of thirty minutes. The day shift had already begun, but he knew nobody would mind if he was a little late. So James walked out of his office and gave the others an easy wave before heading back to the pink bedroom, where his overnight bag had spilled its contents all over one of the beds.

He still wasn't sure what he'd be doing today and spent a little too long debating between the two sets of clothes he'd brought with him. If he was going to be in the state forest, the jeans would be his best bet. But if he was going to be interviewing about the possession or the apparent true-crime podcast notes currently sitting on his desk, shouldn't he look like a professional? Why was this suddenly the hardest decision he was making today?

After three minutes of staring dully at the two piles of clothes in front of him, James grabbed a towel and went to the bathroom. He then realized as he got in the shower that not only had he never made a decision, he hadn't brought any clothes into the bathroom with him.

Oh well, too late now.

The water was blistering hot for once and James took his time, standing under the stream as he thought vaguely about everything and nothing at the same time. They had a lot to do today, but it was under control. With careful planning, they were maybe one or two more team members away from him having a semi-reasonable work schedule. Adding Graham to the team loosened them up somewhat, especially now that he was done with training. The training system had wrapped up in mid-November, about a month ago. So now Graham was a fully-fledged member of the team and could take on any tasks he needed to.

Though, as desperate as James was for more people, he was going to apply Bradley for that northern Maine position himself if he had to sit through a meeting like that again. McGovern was being shockingly reasonable. Sure, he was Foundation, and his expectations were high for the support that they gave. But he wasn't the same guy who had put off sending James his training materials for a month and a half.

No, that guy must have gotten promoted.

He stayed under the water for longer than he'd planned, letting his hair fall into his eyes as the spray dripped down his face. Finally, he reluctantly turned the water off and got out of the shower. The cold air rushed in as soon as he opened the curtain and, swearing under his breath, James grabbed his towel and quickly dried off. As he ran the towel over his arms, he frowned at how thin they were. Apparently, the weeks of rushed workouts were catching up with him. He'd need to get back on his full weight training or his biceps were going to shrink even more. And it wasn't like he was a bodybuilder to begin with.

Oh right, he'd forgotten his clothes in the bedroom. It was only one room down the hall, but the bathroom didn't have a door directly into it. They should really get on that, shouldn't they? He couldn't be the only person to make this mistake. Hoping no one was in the hallway to witness this, James wrapped the towel around his waist and walked out the door.

Only to nearly bump into Amelia. "Oh, sorry!" he said, holding up his hands to let her by.

"Sorry," she echoed, pulling on her coat as she moved to the side. "Hey, I'm going to take the cryptid case now. Sound good?"

That solved case number one of three. "Sure," he said. "It seems like it's just getting his statement, so don't worry about going into the woods."

"I think I need to go check the space. But from the way he described it, it's right off the road," Amelia said. "So I'll just drive by on my way back after and see if anything about it jumps out at me."

"Want some backup?"

Amelia shook her head. "No, just stay on the phones," she said.

"No problem," James said. "Beyond that, we've got the possession in Sterling and whatever the hell is happening over in Ashburnham. Did you see that case file?"

"You mean the murder scene?" Amelia asked. "Yeah, I was eating breakfast when I got to that part. How is that possibly ours?"

"It's two members of the same family, both dead in freak accidents," James said. "I'm going to see if the Foundation has anything else to share, but I'm thinking maybe it's a curse. That's the only thing that would fit the situation, at least as far as I can tell. Demon deal, maybe? But that's a stretch."

"Yeah, this seems small-time for a demonic thing," Amelia said. "But maybe. It's just weird that it's one of ours, though."

"I'll meet with everybody else while you're gone," James said. "We can go over the other two cases and then split the team up to tackle them."

"Just don't forget to get dressed first," Amelia said with a smirk

Right, he was having this impromptu meeting in a towel. "Yeah," James said, glancing around to see if anyone else was there. "Yeah, I'll do that."

As he glanced toward the living room, Madelyn was walking up the stairs from the front door. She reached the top, looked down the hallway at them, and nodded. "Morning, boss," she said, deadpan.

James rolled his eyes. "Alright, I'm going," he said, then walked into the bedroom.

* * *

A few minutes later, he was dressed and presentable, having chosen the slacks and gray button-down shirt. As he walked out of the pink bedroom, Madelyn was walking out of the gray one across the hall. "Morning," James said.

"Hi."

An idea hit him just as he was about to walk past her. "Hey, can I talk to you for a sec?"

"Sure."

He motioned for her to come into the pink bedroom, then closed the door behind them. "What's up?" Madelyn asked, sitting down on the neatly made bed next to the one James had claimed.

Madelyn was young, just about the same age as Amelia, and small with dark hair and dark eyes. She was Amelia's housemate and had joined the Foundation on her referral years earlier. A couple years ago, she'd been involved in a serious accident on the job, and the scars still lingered on both her face and the careful way she moved. But despite all that, she was still bright and enthusiastic about the work.

"Do you know if Amelia's changed her mind about having her own team?" James asked.

Madelyn looked surprised, like this wasn't at all what she'd expected to hear from him. "Not that I know of?" she said. "But I don't think she was really thinking about it happening anytime soon. Why?"

James sat down next to her and ran a hand down his face. "So, the captaincy is opening at one of the New Hampshire branches," he said. "Like, right over the border. I mentioned it to her, and she seemed like she wasn't happy at the thought of it?"

"What do you mean?"

He thought back to the hesitant look on Amelia's face a couple of hours earlier. "I don't know," he said. "It's probably nothing. I just wanted to make sure that I hadn't missed something big, you know? Like, if she'd decided she was going to quit the Foundation or something."

Madelyn laughed. "I don't think Amelia has any plans to quit the Foundation," she said. "She's told me more than once that we're moving to that retirement home together."

Right, the Foundation retirement home for ghost hunters who had managed to keep going into old age. Up until James became captain, he hadn't been a hundred percent sure that it wasn't some urban legend. But not only was it real, he'd actually had to stop by there after a trip to the Boston headquarters back in November.

It had been a pretty nice place.

"So you're sure?" James asked.

Madelyn shrugged and nodded, her short hair bobbing around her head. "As I can be," she said. "If she hasn't told either of us, either it's something serious or she's just being cautious. Becoming captain is a big deal, you know that."

And James hadn't had a chance to be cautious about it. Instead, as the shock of Robin's betrayal and death were still wearing off, the Foundation had handed him the keys and wished him the best of luck. But she was right.

"Okay," James said. "Thanks. I was hoping I hadn't put my foot in it. Like, maybe she'd decided already and told me, but I was too distracted to listen."

"You think she'd let you be distracted?" Madelyn laughed.

"Nope."

He stood up, and Madelyn followed, carefully lowering herself onto the floor. James stood off to the side as she caught her balance. He felt better as they left the bedroom a moment later and headed out to meet the rest of the team.

Chapter 4

Gabriella and Graham were in by now and both gave him a wave from where they were sitting around the coffee table. "Sorry I'm late," Gabriella said. "There was something going on in Fitchburg, and the traffic was just clearing up while I was on my way over."

"Bradley said the same thing. Don't worry about it," James said.

Gabriella glanced over at Bradley, who was working on a slideshow for their meeting. "You live in Fitchburg too?" she asked.

He shrugged, not looking up from his work. James waited to see if there was some snarky comment coming, but nothing did. Gabriella looked like she was trying not to be insulted and he couldn't help the ridiculous little bit of pride at seeing both sides of this interaction. Bradley hadn't said anything terrible and Gabriella hadn't let him get to her.

Yeah, the bar was set in hell, but he'd take the progress.

He walked over to where Bradley was working and pulled out the computer chair next to him. "Need anything?" he asked.

"Space?"

Now it was James's turn to ignore him. "Amelia's got the state forest under control on her own, so we just need to do Sterling and Ashburnham. I was thinking you could do Sterling with Graham while I bring Gabriella with me. Madelyn can cover comms for both until Amelia gets back. It should only be a short overlap."

Bradley hesitated, then nodded. "Yeah, fine," he said.

Graham had been Bradley's college professor at some point in the past couple of years. James knew that Bradley still felt awkward about that dynamic, even though they were on equal footing in the Foundation It was a poorly kept secret that Bradley was completing his bachelor's degree around his work at the Foundation, but he never talked about it. The only reason James knew was because Amelia had slipped up while asking James to adjust the schedule.

James knew there was nothing to be ashamed of, but he wasn't about to have that conversation with Bradley. So instead, he just kept his mouth shut and scheduled Bradley around his on-campus classes.

"Let me know when the slideshow is done and I'll get us started."

Bradley typed something into a slide. "It's done."

"Thanks."

James stood up. "Alright, let's get going," he said. "We've got two cases to focus on today. Amelia's out on the third, which, God willing, is just a statement and a quick glance in the state forest to see if anyone's come out to play. We'll be splitting into two groups to settle these. I'll hand it over to Bradley for the overview."

He pulled down the screen, and a second later, Bradley's slideshow was on the projector. "First, Sterling," Bradley said.

He clicked on the screen and a picture of a smiling ghost appeared. Then, as it faded, the smile became a frown. "Possession," Bradley said. "So this family is pretty sure that their grandfather is either possessed or strongly influenced by something paranormal. It's certainly a theory."

The details of the case appeared on the screen with what looked like the turn of a page. James wasn't sure where Bradley had learned these ridiculous PowerPoint tricks, but if it was one of the few things in this world that made the man happy, then whatever. "They're saying they hear him late at night, talking to people who aren't there," Bradley continued. "The Foundation says that they've done a full medical workup on him and everything seems fine. He insists he's talking to demons."

"Do we do demons?" Graham asked.

Bradley nodded. "If they show up."

"We investigate," James said. "But demons are more Father McEnerney's deal. So if we see solid signs of demonic activity, the case is immediately transferred."

"That's convenient," Graham said.

"Yeah, the Foundation doesn't fuck around when it comes to demons," James said. "It's priests and specially trained staff on those."

Bradley clicked through to the next slide, which showed a smiling old man standing over a towering birthday cake. "This is Henry Carr, the subject of the alleged possession. Family man with three daughters and a wife. The report says they're all very close according to the daughter that brought this to the Foundation."

"That's nice," James said.

Bradley shrugged. "Sure. Anyway, his behavior is off-kilter and there are no medical reasons for it. They're Catholic, so..."

He let the thought trail off, but James had been raised in a big Catholic family, so he could fill in the gaps. And as long as all the medical aspects had already been covered, this should be a straightforward case.

"Bradley and Graham are going to take that one," James said. "You'll interview the family members, try to get some readings in the rooms where he stays. Graham, were there training modules on this?"

"On demons?" Graham asked with raised eyebrows. "Uh, no."

That was a silly oversight on the Foundation's part. Gabriella awkwardly raised her hand. "I didn't have anything about demons either."

Great. "Alright," James said, hoping he didn't sound like his impatience was directed toward them. "Graham, just follow Bradley's lead. Um, we might have some resources somewhere in the building."

"We have some very basic things in the filing cabinet," Bradley said, motioning toward the old filing cabinet that was buried behind the worn couch, beside the collapsing plywood shelf that made up their branch library. "But nothing in depth. Is there anything in the collection in your office?"

James glanced at Gabriella. Robin had left behind a collection of very old, worn-out reference books. She'd been organizing and analyzing the books in his office over the past few weeks, but they hadn't had a chance to talk about it. "Yeah," Gabriella said, face turning pink under their scrutiny. "I found some. They're pretty creepy."

"Can you show Bradley where they are?" James asked.

"In your office?"

"What kinds of secrets do you think I have in there?" James said with a laugh. "Yeah, just grab them and then come back."

She got up and went into the office, hesitating just slightly at the door. Bradley followed, looking to all the world like James had just sent him on a pointless quest that would likely end in death.

As they disappeared into the office, James looked at Graham and Madelyn. "Alright, so Graham, that's going to be your focus. Mads, are you up for double comms for a little while?"

She shrugged. "I mean, these cases seem simple enough."

"Great, thanks. Amelia will be back in a little while. Then she can join you and you can split the teams."

A moment later, Gabriella and Bradley were back, each carrying a handful of books. James squinted at them through the dust floating off the volumes. "All of those?"

"Yeah," Gabriella said. "There's even more still in there."

They both set their stacks of books on the dining room table and James cringed a little as the dust flew up into their faces. Gabriella coughed and waved it away while Bradley closed his eyes and ducked to the side.

"I can go through these ones later, but I won't get to it until tomorrow at the earliest," Bradley said, sitting back down at his computer.

"It's okay, I've taken notes already," Gabriella said.

James couldn't help the satisfaction he felt as Bradley looked up at her in surprise. And clearly, based on the smile on her face, Gabriella couldn't either. "You've read them?" Bradley asked.

"Yeah."

"All of them?"

"I've got about two volumes left to go through, but almost."

Bradley glanced over at James, who gave him a little nod, trying hard not to smirk. "Huh," he said, turning back to Gabriella.

"I'll show you my notes," Gabriella said. "Are you thinking about using them for training materials? To go with the modules the Foundation sent?"

Now Bradley looked around like he might have gotten dropped into an alternate universe. "Um, yeah," he said, clearly caught off guard. "Yeah, I was."

James could watch Gabriella being smoothly professional all day. "Great," she said. "I'll show you what I've got. It'll convert easily."

"Okay. Um, thanks."

Gabriella turned to James, who winked at her. Bradley didn't see, since he'd turned back to the computer by this point, but he seemed thrown off course. The mouse skittered across the screen up on the projector as he found his place in the presentation.

"That's it," he said, clicking on the screen again.

The cheerful cartoon ghost appeared again against a black screen. "Great," James said. "So that's going to be Brad and Graham. What do you have on the Delinsky case?"

"Delinsky?" Bradley said. Then his eyes widened. "Shit, no, not yet. I swear I..."

James didn't know what was weirder, the fact that Bradley didn't have the case prepared, or that he actually seemed flustered. Maybe there was something he'd need to address, but that could wait until later. "That's fine," he said. "Hang on, let me grab the notes and I'll take it from here."

He got up and hurried into his office, noting the dirt on the floor in front of the bookcase where the demon encyclopedia had been. But he'd clean it up later. They needed to wrap up this meeting first. So he grabbed the case file off his desk and hurried back out.

"Update came through," Bradley said, handing him a piece of paper as he walked back into the living room.

Amelia must have wrapped up her case and sent in the follow-up report. But as James glanced at the paper, his stomach sank. When he looked up, all the others were watching him curiously.

"What now?" Graham asked.

James shook his head. "Sorry, it's just an update on the case I was about to share with you all. I couldn't figure out exactly why they were sending it this way. But apparently, it is definitely one of ours."

"The murder one?" Bradley asked with a frown.

"Yeah," he said. "Delinsky. So I guess we're starting from zero on that one, anyway."

Bradley scowled at him, but James just turned to the others. "Okay, so the other case on the docket is because of a couple of strange deaths in one family."

Gabriella winced. "That's rough," she said.

"Yeah," James agreed.

Both were from the same large family and he couldn't help applying the facts of the case to their own. If it were his uncle and aunt, for instance, who had died, he wouldn't be so blasé about it. So he'd make sure to treat this one with the same respect.

"I'll warn you, the photos are pretty graphic," James said. "But we've got two unexplained deaths and one survivor who saw something weird."

Bradley's head shot up at this, and James nodded. "Yeah, that's the update," he said.

"Shit."

"What's going on?" Madelyn asked.

"Two brothers in the same family. Um, if you've ever shopped at Delinsky's, this is that family."

Delinsky's was an upscale clothing store with shops up and down the East Coast. James hadn't put the pieces together before right now as he looked at the new report. Which made sense, considering most of his clothes came from Walmart and Goodwill. But this still added an additional layer to it all.

"So the first victim is Jim Delinsky, age fifty-three. His body was found hanging in the barn behind the family's Ashburnham summer cottage yesterday," James said. "Um, his head was found in the rafters on the other side of the barn."

"Excuse me?" Graham said calmly, despite a nauseated expression on his face.

"Yeah."

"Well, fuck." Graham let out a long breath. "So we're assuming it's not a suicide?"

Don't laugh, don't laugh. James took a deep breath and let it out slowly. "No," he said. "No, we're not thinking that's a possibility."

"Does the Foundation have any thoughts on what did it?" Gabriella asked, looking equally sick.

"Now they do, but I'll get to that in a moment," James said. "There's also his brother, Robert Delinsky, age sixty. His body was found the same morning, along the train tracks in Ashburnham. The body was also in rough shape, like it had been hit by a train."

"Is there any reason why it wouldn't have been?" Bradley asked.

"Because those tracks have been out of commission for a decade."

"So let me get this straight," Madelyn said, holding up a hand. "We've got two brothers, both gruesomely killed the same day in implausible ways?"

"Nailed it."

"And what's the update?" Bradley asked.

"Rita Delinsky, age forty-five," James said, reading from the printout. "She was found alive and conscious, but badly injured on the ice on the lake beside their summer cottage. She says she doesn't remember how she got out there, but she saw a figure on the ice beside her."

"Does she remember getting injured?" Graham asked.

James shrugged. "This is all I have to go on. The family is working with the Foundation and they want whatever is happening to be resolved quickly. So they clearly think there's a paranormal aspect to it. Which, looking at it right now, that's pretty obvious."

"Curse," Bradley said. "I still think it carries all the hallmarks of a family curse."

"It's likely," James said. "And that's what the Foundation is leaning toward. Though the figure part is new and doesn't quite fit the usual standard of a family curse."

"A new curse then?" Gabriella asked.

"That's what I was thinking," James said. "Either way, Gabs, you and I are going to be interviewing Rita Delinsky later today at the hospital, then the other family members over at the cottage."

"So, by 'cottage,'" Gabriella started. "Are we talking, like, an actual little cottage or a rich person's mansion that's called a cottage to be cute?"

"I think we can both take a wild guess," James said with a laugh. "But we'll find out when we get there."

He looked at the gathered group. "Alright," he said. "So Gabs and I are going to be heading to the hospital, then Ashburnham. Bradley and Graham, you're going to Sterling. Madelyn, you're holding things down here. Any questions?"

Everybody shook their heads. "Alright," he said. "I figure we get going shortly. But I don't have anything else to add."

The others started to scatter. "Bradley, you got a sec?" he asked before Bradley could take off.

"Not really."

"It'll just be a minute."

"Fine."

James started walking to his office, trying not to look back to see if Bradley would follow. Apparently, the faked confidence worked, because Bradley reluctantly stood up and walked into the office behind him.

"Look," he said as James closed the door. "If this is about the Delinsky presentation-"

"Not just that," James said. "Though, is everything okay?"

"Fine."

God, he didn't know what else he expected from this conversation. But he was the captain, so it was his job to have it. "It's just not like you to forget," James said. "I'm not, like, mad or anything. Obviously. But if there's something going on-"

"There's not."

"If there's something going on," James repeated, ignoring the interruption. "You can tell me and we'll work it out."

"There's nothing going on," Bradley said. "Is there anything else?"

Yep, like having a heart-to-heart with a brick. Fine, whatever, he couldn't work miracles. "Yeah, actually."

"Great."

Bradley's tone made James want to end the meeting now. "I wanted to ask you," he started, keeping his voice low again as he glanced over to make sure the door was closed. "Do you know if Amelia changed her mind about wanting to become captain?"

"You're resigning?"

James blinked at him, stunned both by the fact that it was even a possibility and that it had apparently startled Bradley. "What?" he said. "No, I'm not. But that Hillsborough position is opening, and I mentioned it to her. I thought she'd be excited, but she just, like, closed up when I told her. So I wondered if maybe I'd missed something."

"I haven't heard anything," Bradley said.

"Okay."

So maybe it was nothing. And if he kept asking around, Amelia would find out and get pissed. He was just overreacting and making a big deal out of nothing.

"Is there anything else?"

"No, that's it."

Bradley turned to leave. "So you'd miss me?" James said before he could get to the door.

Bradley glanced over his shoulder. "What?"

"If I'd said yes, I was resigning. You'd miss me?"

"I'd welcome the quiet."

"You'd stand outside my window with a boombox, wouldn't you? Playing 'Spooky Scary Skeletons' until I agreed to come back?"

Bradley's mouth twitched, but he just glared at James. "I have to go," he said.

"Alright, you go see a boy about a demon. Don't worry, I'll be here when you get back."

Bradley swore under his breath as he swept out of the office, but James was amused to see he was turning red. After a beat, he headed back to his desk, then grabbed his car keys and went out to the living room, where Gabriella and Madelyn were standing. "Gabs, are you ready to go, or do you need more time?" James asked.

"I'm ready," Gabriella said. "Let me get my bag."

Graham came out of the kitchen, pulling on his coat. "James," he said. "Thank you so much for riling up Bradley just before I'm stuck in the car with him. Truly, I'm in your debt."

Whoops. "My bad," James said. "Um, I'll buy you a beer tonight."

"Speaking of," Graham started as he zipped his neat black coat. "Chris wanted to talk to both of us tonight. He said it's important."

That could only mean one of two things. Either he wanted to move someone in or he was moving out. Neither of which were particularly great options for James and Graham. And looking at Graham's grimace, James could tell he was thinking the same thing.

"I'll get a six-pack," James edited. "I'm home tonight, but I'm going to bed early. So it better not be one of his three AM chats."

"Same here," Graham said. "I told him I was pretty sure we would both be home, so he should be reasonable."

Or at least as reasonable as Chris got. He was their harmless, though extremely odd, third roommate. He was at least eight years older than James and had provided good references, but as little information as legally possible on his background when he'd moved in with them.

"Graham, are you coming?"

Bradley's impatient voice came up the stairs, and Graham rolled his eyes. "Thanks a lot," he muttered.

"A twelve-pack," James promised.

"I already gave final grades last year. I have no power anymore."

Graham's voice was almost silent, but James still looked toward the stairs in case Bradley heard him. God, if Bradley found out James knew. Though he knew Graham and James were housemates, so maybe he thought James already knew. But no, he would have said something. Oh, James was never going to tell him anyway, so it didn't matter.

Graham hurried down the steps and the two of them left a second later. James turned to Madelyn, who was getting herself situated at the computer. "You're still good for both?" he confirmed as he pulled on his own coat.

"Yeah," she said. "As long as things don't get too complicated on either end, I'm fine. And when Amelia gets back, it can get as complicated as it needs to."

"Great," James said as Gabriella came into the room. "Alright, we're out."

Chapter 5

From the look the nurse gave James as he said he was here to speak to Mrs. Delinsky, he knew he was in for it. The nurse picked up the phone, but it was easy to figure out which room in the sterile hospital hallway was hers, even before her harried-looking nephew came down the hall looking for them. Hers was the one that was surrounded by people in expensive suits. The sound of someone yelling hoarsely carried through the air as a white-faced nurse hurried out of the room as well.

The nephew, a tall man a little younger than James and nicely tanned for mid-December, stopped at the nurse's station. The stress dropped from his face as he looked James over. "Are you from the Foundation for Paranormal Studies?"

"Yeah," James said, holding out a hand to shake. "I'm James McManus and this is my cousin, Gabriella McManus. We're here to interview Mrs. Delinsky."

"Terrific," the young man said, taking James's hand in a firm, practiced handshake. "It's nice to meet you. I'm Zach Delinsky, Rita's nephew. Thank you for coming. We're hoping to keep this as discreet as possible."

Zach Delinsky held himself with the confidence of someone who came from money. His teeth were sparkling white as he smiled at James for a beat longer, then turned to give Gabriella a quick handshake as well. "Cousin, huh?"

He looked back over at James with a charmingly raised eyebrow and expectant smile. James was about to say something in response, but the sound of a shouted lecture was still coming from the hospital room. As they walked toward it, James tried not to groan. But clearly, Zach could see what was going on because he gave James a wry smile.

"Yeah," he said. "Aunt Rita does not like being told what to do. And with everything that's happened, tension's been pretty high, you know?"

"Of course," James said. "We're sorry for your loss."

"Thank you," Zach said. "My uncles were two of the worst things to happen to our family. But I appreciate the sentiment."

James and Gabriella exchanged a look, but said nothing. Zach either didn't notice or didn't care as he led them through the group of nicely dressed men and women and headed into the hospital room.

An older nurse with a lined face was standing by the door as they came in. "Ma'am, just let us know if you need anything," she said, voice flatly professional as she nodded toward Mrs. Delinsky, who was lying in the hospital bed.

"I won't need anything from you," Rita Delinsky said, voice raspy and ice cold.

The nurse rolled her eyes at James as she walked out, and he grimaced in sympathy at her. This was going to be fun.

"Mrs. Delinsky?" he said, taking another step in.

"Who the fuck are you?"

"Aunt Rita, these are the people from the Foundation. They're here to talk to you about–" Zach's voice dropped as he glanced toward the door. "–about what happened."

"Great, it's about time."

Rita Delinsky had her leg in a cast and was hooked up to a few monitors beside the bed, but her eyes looked clear and alert as she narrowed them at James. He knew what she saw. He was scruffy, unshaven, and tired-looking. And normally he thought nothing of that. But right now, he could feel her judgment and just wanted to be done with this.

"I'm James McManus, the captain of the North Worcester County branch," he said. "And this is Gabriella, one of my associates."

Rita Delinsky looked at Gabriella. "What are you, seventeen?" she said. "No, I need professionals."

"We are professionals, ma'am," James said. "We report directly to the

Foundation for Paranormal Studies in Boston. Could you please tell us what happened this morning?"

"I have no idea," Rita said, looking up at the white tiles on the ceiling. "I woke up on the ice outside the cottage."

"Were you spending the night there?" James asked.

"No," Rita replied. "I was at home in Wellesley last night."

"Wait," James said. "So you fell asleep in Wellesley and woke up in Ashburnham."

"Yes," Rita answered tersely. "With four broken bones and a concussion."

James winced. "I'm sorry," he said. "Um, can you tell me what you remember?"

"That's all there is," Rita snapped. "I went to bed in Wellesley. When I woke up, I was cold and in pain. I opened my eyes and saw a figure standing over me."

"What did they look like?" Gabriella asked.

"Formless," Rita replied.

For a second, the harsh mask dropped away, and James could see genuine fear in her eyes. "It was like a person made of smoke. It got close to my face, but I couldn't see any features. And then it vanished."

James mentally ran through the possibilities. Shadow person. Or maybe that mischief spirit from Halloween, or one of its kin. But mischiefs didn't go around shattering people and transporting them fifty miles west of their beds, at least in James's experience.

"Anyway, someone was trespassing on my family's land and called the police, who came and got me," Rita said.

"They were taking a walk in the woods," Zach clarified, giving James a long-suffering look.

"On our land," Rita snapped. "They're lucky I didn't call the cops on them."

James was grateful for all the practice he had at keeping his face neutral because he needed every bit of it right now. "Then what happened?" he asked.

"Then nothing," Rita replied. "They brought me here. And whatever that is, it killed my brothers yesterday. This isn't natural and we're paying the Foundation a lot of money to solve this. You're supposed to be protecting us."

James and Gabriella looked at each other. "We're not bodyguards..." James started.

"No, those gentlemen outside are," Zach said.

James looked outside. The people in suits that he'd assumed were family members were still milling around in the hallway. But as he looked closer, he saw a comms device in one of their ears.

So there was security involved. Good of the Foundation to let him know.

"Right," James said. "We're going to be talking to some of your other family members over at the, um, the cottage later today, too. The Foundation has us out here to collect data and figure out how to stop this."

"What is it?" Rita demanded, that fear sneaking into her voice again. "What could do this?"

"We don't know yet," James admitted. "We're still getting all the information. But my team will be working on it along with the main branch in Boston, so we'll keep you updated. And in the meantime, the folks out there will get you set up with all the protections we have available."

"I guess it'll have to do," Rita muttered. "Now leave. I'm tired. I'm going to rest now."

"Right," James said. "Thanks for your time. We'll be in touch. Um, take care."

Rita had closed her eyes, but she opened them enough to glare at him before closing them again. Zach motioned for James and Gabriella to follow him out the door.

James made eye contact with one of the bodyguards as he walked past, a bald bulldog of a man, who gave him a wink. James smiled and nodded back, then hurried after Zach.

"Sorry about my aunt," Zach said. "Even on her good days, she's a nightmare. They all are."

"Don't worry about it," James said. "We're used to dealing with all kinds of people."

"So you're heading to The Cottage from here?"

Zach pronounced it in a way that James just knew it was capitalized. "Sure are," James said.

"Good. The rest of my family is there now. I'll be going over later, so take my card. Call me if you need anything."

Zach handed James a business card, and he took it without a second thought, as though he took business cards all the time. "Thanks," he said, slipping it into his pocket.

"It's nice to have you here. You seem like you know what you're doing."

It had been a little while since someone had said that to James, and he wasn't quite sure what to say in return. But Zach just gave him another brilliant smile. "I'll see you soon."

Zach walked back toward the room, leaving James and Gabriella to head toward the elevators.

"Wow, she was a treat," James muttered as the elevator doors slid shut behind them.

"Seriously," Gabriella said. "She's lucky she's not dead, and she's still complaining?"

She let out a long breath, then raised her eyebrows at James. "So, are you going to call him?" she asked.

James had pulled out his phone to check for any missed calls from Headquarters. "Hmm?" he asked, scrolling through a text from Amelia confirming everything was fine at the State Forest.

"Zach."

"I mean, if we need anything, I guess. I'll see how it goes at this cottage, though."

There was silence for a little too long as he responded to Amelia's text. He looked up to see Gabriella looking at him, eyebrows raised.

"What?"

"Are you serious?"

James shrugged, lifting his hands in frustration. "What are you talking about?"

"He was flirting with you, dumbass."

"No, he wasn't."

Gabriella looked at him, shaking her head in apparent disappointment. "Did you seriously not notice?" she asked as the doors opened on the ground floor.

"Notice what?" James said, walking out of the elevator and into the lobby. "He was not flirting with me. He was offering help if we needed it on a case."

"Oh yeah, and all of our sources are so charming and so willing to help."

"If you think he was so charming, you call him."

"He didn't look at me twice," Gabriella said.

"He wasn't flirting with me."

"What's the problem?" Gabriella asked as the automatic doors opened and they headed out into the parking lot. "Is it because he's a guy?"

"Of course not," James snapped, looking around for his car. "But this wasn't flirting. All he did was hand me his card and offer help. Wait, is that how you and Elliot got started?"

He could almost hear her roll her eyes as he spotted his car and started toward it. "Do you have any cash?" he asked. "I have to pay for parking, and I think the credit card machine here is usually broken."

Chapter 6

James had called it with the Cottage with a capital C. As they pulled off the main road and down a winding, neatly kept path, he could see the top of the building through the trees ahead of them. A sign along the side of the road read, in elegant, sloping print, "The Cottage at Delinsky Cove."

"Delinsky Cove?" Gabriella said, squinting at the sign with a disgusted shake of her head. "Are you kidding me?"

James rolled his eyes. The forest was thick, but felt curated in a way that told him someone spent a lot of time designing it to look natural. Then the road curved, and they were coming up on a mansion. It was a beautiful building, but there was no way anyone in their right mind would call this a cottage. It had to have at least three stories, and there were pillars around the front door. From here, he could see a spacious porch wrapping around the side and into the backyard. The yard was a vast slope of impeccably cared for grass that led to a small beach against what was clearly a private lake. It looked a lot like the one the aunts used to bring them to as kids, but James knew no one was coming out of this one with leeches on their legs.

The water was frozen now, and he could see police tape fluttering on the ice. Further down the yard, he saw the barn where Jim Delinsky and his head had parted ways. There was tape along the entrance there, plus muddy tracks through the snow where the investigators had been. But even that couldn't completely detract from the peacefulness of the so-called Delinsky Cove.

Gabriella let out a low whistle as they pulled into the massive driveway. "Damn."

James shrugged and laughed. "Looks like a cottage to me," he said.

They got out of their car and walked across the parking lot-sized driveway. Several cars were parked along the edge of the precisely trimmed grass, a couple of Mercedes-Benzes, and what looked like a lovingly restored Porsche from the seventies. James's car looked even worse than usual parked against this backdrop, but whatever. They weren't here to impress anyone.

James walked up the marble steps to the porch and rang the doorbell. It echoed somewhere deep in the house. Then he and Gabriella waited in silence until he heard footsteps approaching on the other side. A moment later, the door opened and an old woman peeked out, narrowing her eyes as she looked at them. "Yes?" she said. "Who are you?"

"Hi, I'm James McManus from the Foundation for Paranormal Studies," he said.

No matter how long he did this job, and how smooth his delivery was, James always felt like an asshole introducing himself like that. Like he should have a cape and some Criss Angel moves or something, as he said it. He half expected the woman to close the door in his face, but instead, she opened it further.

"We've been expecting you," she said. "I'm Maria, Mrs. Delinsky's personal assistant."

"We were just at the hospital talking with her," James said.

"She told you what happened?" Maria asked.

"Yeah," James said. "We're here to talk to more family members and get the pieces to put together what's going on."

"You better do it soon," Maria said, her voice low. "They're panicking in there, no matter how many bodyguards your Foundation sends."

"James!"

James looked over to see Father McEnerney, the priest consultant they worked with on a regular basis, walking through the front foyer of the house. He was a little older than James, with a boyish face and black hair in need of a cut. But in his Roman collar and black suit, he was all business.

"Father," James said, reaching out to shake. "I take it you're one of the bodyguards?"

Father McEnerney laughed. "I guess you could say that."

He turned to Gabriella. "Gabriella," he said. "Good to see you. Sadie and her son told me to thank you for everything."

Gabriella shuffled a little awkwardly. "It was nothing," she said.

No, it was something. Gabriella had risked her life going after the mischief entity a couple of months ago, and her quick thinking had led it right into their trap. He knew she thought it was no big deal, but James refused to see her actions as just part of the job.

"So, what are you doing here?" James asked.

"The Foundation's pulling out all the stops on this one," Father McEnerney said as Maria walked away. "I've been blessing every inch of this place. There are multiple agents here to guard the family and we've got protections up in all entrances. Whatever this thing is, it's powerful enough to kill two men and compel a woman halfway across the state."

"Do you have any ideas?"

"Curse," Father McEnerney said immediately. "It has to be a curse. I don't have any extrasensory abilities to speak of, but Boston sent a couple of mediums out here and they both agree."

"That's what we're thinking too," James said.

"Father!" someone, an older man with a gravelly voice, called from the crowded rooms nearby. "Father, you're needed."

"When aren't I needed?" Father McEnerney muttered to James. Then he plastered on his calm priestly face, which James had seen often enough to know it was total shit, and walked out of the room.

He always enjoyed working with Father McEnerney.

"You're here from the Foundation?"

This time, it was a much younger woman's voice. James turned around to see a stunning red-haired woman standing in yet another doorway. "Yes," he said. "We're here from the North Worcester County branch to interview family members."

The woman nodded, all cool professionalism despite the paranormal chaos around her. "Right this way," she said.

Before either of them could say anything, the woman spun around and started down the hallway, her high heels clacking on the cold floor. James and Gabriella hurried to catch up with her.

"I'm glad you're here," the woman said without looking at them. "This has been horrific. What happened to the Delinsky brothers was terrifying, but to have whatever this is drag Mrs. Delinsky out here as well... it's too much."

"You seem calm though," James said.

The slightest smile appeared on the woman's face as she punched a code into a pad mounted beside a dark wooden door. "It's my job," she said.

"You work for the family?"

"I'm Mr. Delinsky's assistant."

The one whose head was ripped off or the victim of the phantom train? James wasn't quite sure what to say. But apparently, his silence said it all.

"Yes, Robert Delinsky was my immediate supervisor," the woman said. "I'm Yasmin, by the way."

"It's nice to meet you, Yasmin," James said. "I'm sorry for your loss."

"Me too," Gabriella added.

Yasmin sighed as the door clicked open. She pulled it aside, revealing another hallway that she ushered them into. "Thank you," she said. "Mr. Delinsky was... a hard man. But he was a person, and no one deserves that."

Interesting. James filed that note away for later. "Is everyone so accepting that this was paranormal?" Gabriella asked.

Yasmin nodded. "As much as they can be," she said. "There are some holdouts, but we've all seen what's happening with our own eyes. And the sooner we accept it, the sooner we can resolve it. Which is what you're here to do."

"We are," James said.

"What is causing this?"

The first sign of any fear was the slight catch in her voice. James shook his head. "I can't say," he replied. "We have some theories, but I need to talk to family members and get more information before we can determine the best way to resolve it."

They walked silently through the lushly carpeted hallway until they reached another door off to the side. "The family wanted to stay on lockdown until things are resolved," Yasmin said. "I don't blame them. But you'll find their representatives here. Good luck."

She unlocked the door and opened it, revealing a wide, brightly lit conference room. The fact that this was in the middle of the so-called Cottage was so jarring that James almost laughed out loud at the sight. But instead, he just smiled at the gathered people inside.

There were five family members in the room. Two elderly men, a woman in her sixties, and two men that were probably in their twenties. They were all looking at James with wary expressions as he and Gabriella stepped inside.

"These are the representatives from the Foundation," Yasmin said, her voice clipped and cool. "They've cleared the checks and want to get as much information from you as possible."

The two young men made eye contact with James and he realized that one of them was a Foundation agent. Wow, they really had pulled out all the stops here. Were there any security agents at any other cases right now?

James nodded hello, waiting for anyone to offer him and Gabriella a seat. But all three of the older people just glared while the youngest man worried at a hangnail beside the agent.

"May I..." he started, gesturing toward the table.

Still looking sour, the two old men nodded toward a couple of empty chairs. Gabriella hesitantly sat down in one while James took the other.

"I'm going to record our conversation if that's alright with you," James said, pulling out his recorder.

"Absolutely not," the woman snapped.

James glanced at her, hand still on the power button. "Excuse me?"

The woman glared at him, her dark red lips thin on her pale face. "There are no recording devices allowed in this room. We hold very secure meetings here and recordings could have a devastating impact on our business."

As could two dead board members, with a third that just got away. "Um, okay," James said. "Gab, do you have a notepad or something?"

Gabriella looked at him. "Right," James said. "Of course. Maybe just use your phone?"

"No phones," the older of the two elderly men said, his voice loud and wavering.

"She's just going to take notes," James said. "We're not recording anything."

"I told you already, no phones, no recording equipment," the woman said. "The Foundation won't let us require NDAs for their people here, which is frankly ridiculous. We can't know for sure that you won't record, and we can't take that risk."

James blinked slowly, looking over at Gabriella, who seemed equally skeptical. This was a clothing store, not INTERPOL. But they weren't going to get any information this way, so he just shook his head. "Fine," he said. "Does anyone have any paper?"

The agent looked at him with a hint of amusement in his eyes. Clearly, this guy had been here the entire time, and this shit wasn't new. The other young man wordlessly slid a legal pad over to James.

"Do you mind taking notes?" he asked Gabriella.

"Nope," she said, pulling a pen out of her pocket. "Got it."

"Right."

He turned to the three Delinskys. "Could I get your names?" he asked.

The woman rolled her eyes. "Ms. Delinsky," she said.

"First name?"

"You don't need that."

Oh, for Christ's sake. James was about to just move on when he heard a small voice behind him. "Mom..."

He turned and saw the young man looking at the woman. "Mom, this isn't a job interview. This is a murder investigation," the man said. "Can you please just work with him? It killed Dad. What if that thing comes back for us?"

His voice trembled, and James felt a pang of sympathy. This kid couldn't have been any older than twenty. Gabriella clearly felt the same way as she turned and gave him a comforting smile.

The woman sighed. "Fine," she said. "I'm Sarah Delinsky."

Gabriella scribbled her name down as James turned to the other two. "And you?"

Both glared at him, but finally, the older one shook his head. "Theodore Delinsky."

"James Harrington."

He turned to the young man. "And you?"

"Also James. James Delinsky."

"Lots of Jameses," Gabriella murmured as she took notes.

"I'm James as well," James said. "And this is Gabriella. I'm the captain of the North Worcester County branch of the Foundation, and Gabriella is here as my assistant."

Those words never would fit comfortably in his mouth, would they? The young man was back to fidgeting with a hangnail while the others continued to glare at James.

"Okay, now that we're all introduced, can you tell me what you know?" he asked.

Everyone was quiet for a moment. Then the woman took a breath. "My husband disappeared overnight," she said. "We were at home and when I woke up, he was gone. I got a call from the police out here."

"Where's home?" James asked.

"Back Bay."

A ritzy Boston neighborhood. This fit the pattern with Rita Delinsky, who was spirited away from her home in a wealthy Boston suburb. "Did he show any indication that something might happen?"

"You think my husband committed suicide by going on defunct train tracks and waiting for a ghost train to run him over?" Sarah Delinsky asked, her voice tight.

"No," James said. "But I need to follow every angle, if only to eliminate it as a possibility. What about any plans in this area that he might have kept secret?"

"No, of course not," Sarah said.

"This is the family summer home," James Harrington said, his droning voice immediately grating on James's last nerve. "We keep it active in the winter as well, but nobody spends much time here when it's cold."

This summer home was bigger than three of James's triple-decker apartment building put together. But that wasn't what he was here to judge, so he just nodded as Gabriella marked the information down. "And did he have any enemies?"

"The police already asked this," Sarah said.

"Mom," younger James hissed.

"I know," James said. "But we need all the information we can get. If you can think of someone that would want to hurt your husband and his brother, it could be an enormous help."

"There are always people that want to hurt our family," Sarah said. "We own one of the most successful clothing brands in the United States. And we're very selective about who we work with. Of course there are resentments and enemies. But no one who could do this."

She was remarkably calm, but James could see from the strain around her eyes that she was holding it together for appearances. He tried to pull up some sympathy for her and was almost surprised to find a little to give.

"You will figure this out," Theodore said. "My nephews were the backbone of this family's business. If this gets out, it could ruin us."

"What do you mean?" Gabriella asked.

Sarah glared at her. "Would you want to work for a cursed business?" she asked, voice dripping with condescension.

James held his breath, waiting to see if Gabriella was going to crumple and he'd have to step in. But she just looked evenly at Sarah. "Not particularly."

"There you go. We can't have the public finding out that there is anything otherworldly about this. If I hadn't seen everything I've seen, I wouldn't believe it either. But I want it to be quiet and solved quickly. And God help you both if I see a single thing in the press."

James raised his eyebrows. "Noted," he said.

He stood up and Gabriella followed suit. "Thank you for your time," he said. "I'll be in touch. Our team is going to work alongside the Boston branch to figure out what's going on. In the meantime, keep following the instructions of the security team. They'll keep you safe."

"You're sure?" the young man - James - asked.

James nodded. "Yeah," he said. "They're some of the best in the business. You'll be fine."

He nodded at the others gathered around the table and as he turned toward the door, it opened and Yasmin walked in. "I'll lead you out," she said.

Nobody said goodbye as James and Gabriella followed Yasmin out of the room. She walked them back down the long hallway toward the locked wooden door. "I forgot to give back their legal pad," Gabriella said.

"Keep it," Yasmin said. "Listen, they might not show it, but we appreciate what you're all doing. If the family's not going to acknowledge you, know that the staff will."

She smiled, and James felt that sense of underpaid camaraderie between them. "Thanks," he said.

They were quiet until they got to the front door, then Yasmin opened it and held it for them. "What happens next?" she asked.

"We'll see," James said. "We need to discuss it as a branch and see what other leads we can get from this. But it's top priority, don't worry."

She nodded and gave both of them a small smile as they walked out. Then she closed the door, leaving them standing on the cold entryway.

Chapter 7

A few hours later, James was heading home. The case Graham and Bradley had gone to canvas was, in fact, a demonic possession. Bradley had called Father McEnerney, who had added it to his long to-do list, promising he'd get out there tonight on his way home from Ashburnham. When he found out, James wondered briefly if the priest ever actually slept. He wanted to ask if everything was fine with his workload, but he also didn't have another person to turn to about demonic possession. So he felt like asking would be a bit like adding salt to the wound. And would make him a hypocrite, considering he had just wrapped up a twenty-four-hour shift.

Now here he was, dragging his ass into his apartment, climbing each step to their third-floor unit with strength that was giving out. Finally, he got to the top, opened the door, and went straight over to fall on the couch.

He'd get dinner in a few minutes. He just needed a moment to catch his breath first.

"James."

Chris's voice came from somewhere above him, and James's first instinct was to bat it away. But he opened his eyes and reluctantly answered. "Yeah?"

"Do you know when Graham will be home? I need to talk to both of you."

Dammit, he'd forgotten. Graham was on his way as far as James knew. They'd gotten out at the same time, not that Chris knew they worked together. "Um, soon," he said.

He was saved from having to make awkward small talk by the sound of the front door opening. Graham walked in and from the way he stopped in the doorway, James could see he'd forgotten about this meeting too. If Chris noticed either of their reluctance, he didn't say anything. "Perfect," he said. "I need to talk to both of you."

He motioned for Graham to come in, which he did, eyeing James as he perched on the armrest at the other end of the couch. Chris didn't seem nervous, not that he ever did. But anything that involved him talking to both of them was enough to make James uneasy.

"So listen," Chris said. "I've loved living here. Seriously. But unfortunately, I've realized it's time for me to move on. It's nothing either of you did, I just need to get back out on the road. I'm not the type to stay in one place too long."

Clearly not, since their lease wasn't up for another three months. "When are you leaving?" James asked, keeping his tone one of polite, casual interest and not financial worry.

"Next month," Chris said. "I'm waiting for my van to get back from the shop. And don't worry, I'll help you find a new guy to replace me."

That was a relief? Wasn't it?

"Um, great," James said.

"Yeah, good luck," Graham added, his voice with that same neutral politeness that James heard in his own.

"Thanks, man, thanks," Chris said, looking from one of them to the other. "It's been great. And like I said, I'll ask around. I know there's plenty of guys looking for a room."

That wasn't what James was concerned about. But he just nodded, that vague smile frozen on his face.

Chris wandered out of the room a few minutes later with murmured plans of making dinner. But like usual, he went back to his bedroom. James and Graham stayed in the living room.

"I guess that's basically what I expected," Graham said from where he was now slumped in the crappy maroon armchair left behind by the previous occupant.

"Yeah, same."

"Do we want to go with Chris's choices, or should we try to find someone ourselves?" Graham asked. "I mean, if it's just the two of us, I think I can handle the rent hike until the lease ends. But not permanently."

"Agreed," James said.

"What, you're not raking in the cash as captain?"

James laughed bitterly. "I technically got a raise," he said. "But I'd be pushing my luck too. Let's see what Chris offers up, but we can look around. We'll just have to find the time to, like..."

He trailed off, even the thought of searching for a new housemate too exhausting to contemplate right now. Neither option seemed particularly promising, but he'd have to figure it out. Later. For now, he was going to bed.

* * *

Now that the state forest sighting and the Carr possession had both been shuffled off to their appropriate departments, the entire team was temporarily focused on the Delinsky case until something else arrived. James got to work the next morning at nine to see Amelia and Gabriella sitting in the living room with a pad of paper on the coffee table in front of them. They were deep in conversation and barely looked up to say hello as James walked in.

"What are you doing?" he asked, sitting down at the other end of the couch and peering at the pad, which was covered in notes.

"I've been catching her up on the Cottage visit," Gabriella said. "And explaining what a nightmare those people were."

"They're rich," Amelia said, waving a hand dismissively. "Of course, they won't comprehend the severity of what's happening. They've been protected. Even now, the ones you met yesterday are more concerned about saving their company than..."

She trailed off for a second, her gaze turning toward the window where a light flurry of snow was falling. "Amelia?" James prompted. "You okay?"

"Yeah," she said, turning back to them. "Um, have we talked to anybody who works for them?"

"Like their house staff? Yeah, me and Gabriella met a couple yesterday."

"No, like in their stores. The staff at Delinsky's. Managers, floor staff, the non-corporate ones. The ones most likely to be screwed by business decisions."

James had been contemplating getting a bagel for breakfast before everyone arrived for the day and the work began, but Amelia had something here. Breakfast forgotten, he pulled out his phone and looked up Delinsky's locations. As he did so, an article from last year appeared at the same time as the addresses of the four nearest locations. He opened the link and scanned it quickly.

"Their profits took a hit last year," he said as he read. "I wonder if maybe they made some decisions that ended up screwing some of their employees."

"It seems more likely than a jealous family member, which was my other thought," Amelia said. "We've been looking into any public information about their finances and it doesn't seem like anybody's being edged out of the profits. And the few members of the Delinsky family who are not involved in the clothing shop are doing just fine with their own businesses."

"You did all of that over the night shift?" James asked.

Gabriella shrugged. "It was slow," she said.

"Still."

"So I feel like we should still keep the family in mind, but maybe turn some of our resources toward the stores," Amelia continued. "Especially if they've had to do any layoffs or cut benefits."

"Do you think someone would be so upset by cut benefits that they'd murder their CEO?" James asked.

"I started fighting ghosts for health insurance," Gabriella reminded him.

James thought back to all the times he wanted to quit his job, but couldn't because of the benefits. "Alright, fair," he said. "I want to meet with the entire team before you two leave, if you don't mind sticking around just a little longer."

"I'm on the day shift," Amelia said.

"Same."

James was about to argue that they needed to go home anyway when the door opened and Madelyn slowly stepped inside. Judging from the way she very slowly took off her shoes and inched her way upstairs, James could tell she was having a rough day.

"Madelyn, you don't need to be here if you're hurting," James said as she cautiously hobbled over to the couch.

"I'm fine," she said breathlessly, waving him off. "Don't worry about it."

Looking at her bright red face, he thought maybe he should worry about it. But from the slightly sharp tone of her voice, he could tell that pushing it was going to be a bad idea.

"We're going to have a quick meeting when Bradley and Graham get here," he said instead. "We've got some leads on the Delinsky case and I want us all on it while there's nothing else to worry about."

The door opened again as Amelia was beginning to explain their possibilities, and Bradley and Graham both walked in. They were talking about something that James couldn't catch and he might have imagined it, but Bradley looked almost interested in what Graham was saying. But the conversation ended before they got up the stairs.

"Quick meeting before we all get started," James said as the last two sat down. "I want to do it quickly before Gabs and Amelia take a break. But here's where we stand with the Delinsky case."

He went through everything they'd discussed with the family yesterday, plus what Gabriella and Amelia had considered last night. Finally, after pulling up a list of the four Delinsky's locations within a hundred miles of them, he stopped and took a sip of his ice coffee.

"So, are we leaning more toward the employees or family?" Graham asked.

"Employees," James said. "I'm not ruling out the family entirely, but they all seem comfortable enough and I'm not finding any outcasts in the family in case we are thinking estrangement."

"But we're still focusing on both," Amelia said. "I'm going to take an hour's nap when we're done here, but I say we split the team while we've got all of us available. Save some time."

"Good call," James said. "I'll wrap this up quickly so you two can go get some sleep. I bet we can hit a couple locations today and get some information from the managers there. Amelia, you want to go with me?"

"Yeah, sure."

"Gabs and Bradley, you're going to go back to the Cottage at Delinsky Cove." James made sure to give the name the emphasis it deserved. "There's another set of family members to talk to. Brad, it's a trip. You're going to love it. Mads and Graham, you'll stay here on comms."

Graham looked over at Madelyn, who nodded, then winced. "You okay?" James heard him murmur.

"Yeah," she said back, just as softly.

Graham handed her a throw pillow, which she gripped tightly on her lap. God, James wanted to send her home so badly, but he knew how insulting that would be. "Just do what you can today," he said instead. "And if you want to go rest or anything, please do."

She nodded, looking slightly miserable. James cringed. Had he insulted her anyway? Before he could lodge his foot any further into his mouth, Amelia stood up. "If we're done, I'm gonna head out back."

"Go for it," James said. "I've got plenty to do, so take your time. We'll head out later in the morning."

She and Gabriella headed down the hall toward the bedrooms, leaving James, Bradley, Madelyn, and Graham in the living room. "I'll make coffee," Bradley said, standing up and disappearing into the kitchen.

Bradley's coffee was always oddly thick, but very potent. If James poured in half a gallon of milk, it'd fuel him through the rest of the day. Graham stayed next to Madelyn, but turned to James.

"Did you hear Chris talking in his room last night?" he asked.

James shook his head. "No, like on the phone? That seems pretty normal."

"Yeah, except for the parts where he was getting the cabin set up. With a Wi-Fi dampener."

"He's a weirdo," James said. "Maybe it's part of his whole 'finding himself on the open road' thing."

"True," Graham said. "I don't blame him. I need a vacation too."

"Same," Madelyn said with a shaky laugh as she pulled her legs up onto the couch.

Her heating pad was on the coffee table, so James handed it to her and she plugged it in, setting it into place against her back. "The Foundation can give us all the vacation days in the world," James said. "But they don't staff us enough to use them."

"Do they roll over?" Graham asked.

"Sure do," James said with a grim smile. "I've got almost a hundred days banked. I'm going to tell them to fuck off and use all one hundred at once."

Madelyn laughed again, setting her head back against the throw pillow she'd been holding. "I've got forty. They didn't dare try to make me use sick time or vacation time for my surgeries."

"You can cash them in," James said. "That's what a lot of people do. I'm still holding out hope, though."

"Hope for what?"

Bradley was back, holding two cups of coffee. He handed one to Madelyn, who took it gratefully. Then Bradley jerked his head toward the kitchen. "There's more in there."

James went to the kitchen and tried not to notice how slowly the coffee poured from the carafe. He had a gallon of milk in the fridge that hadn't turned yet, so he poured a healthy amount in as Graham set up his own coffee.

When they got back to the living room, he sat down in his original spot and sipped his drink. "We were talking about vacation time," he said.

"I cash mine in," Bradley said. "It's not worth trying."

Graham looked slightly like he was regretting taking the job right now. "When was the last time any of you took a vacation?" he asked, though judging by his face, he clearly knew the answer.

"Are we counting work trips?" James asked.

"Absolutely not."

James thought back. "God," he said. "I'm honestly not sure. I went away for a few days, um, five years ago?"

Graham looked at the other two. They didn't need to say anything. He turned back and James suddenly felt very pathetic.

"Listen," he said, aware that he sounded defensive. "It's not like I have the money to fly off anywhere for a couple weeks anyway."

"No, but you could take a few days off," Graham said. "Lay on the couch all day. Or, I don't know, pick up a hobby. Do you have any hobbies?"

"Baking," Madelyn replied.

"Dance nights in Boston," Bradley said.

"Netflix," James said.

Then he turned to Bradley. "Wait, what?"

"How many times do I need to tell you I have a life outside of here?" Bradley snapped.

James shook his head. "You astonish me."

"Netflix?" Bradley retorted.

"You just proved my point," Graham said. "James, you need to take a vacation. You all do, but that's just sad."

"I will," James said. "Let's just get through this case, get a new roommate, and then I'll try to figure out when I can have a day off."

"A day isn't a vacation," Graham said. "Back me up here, guys."

"You could use a break," Madelyn admitted.

James considered mentioning that she'd refused to go home and rest, but that felt like lobbing a grenade into an otherwise lighthearted argument. "Fine," he said. "I'll take a few. Happy?"

"Always."

"Not until after we get a replacement roommate, though," James said. "I'm not dealing with that during my first actual vacation in five years."

"I'll accept it," Graham said, holding out a hand to shake.

James took his hand, feeling like maybe he'd just fallen into a trap.

Chapter 8

A few hours later, James and Amelia were in the van, heading toward a mall about thirty-five minutes south of Headquarters. The sky was slate gray as they drove down the highway, but there was frost sparkling on the last lingering leaves that refused to fall from the trees. James looked up at the leaves as they blurred by the passenger side window.

"So you're thinking we should hit two stores?" Amelia asked.

"Yeah, at least for now," James replied. "We've got this one just south of Worcester. And then, from there, we might as well loop up and around to the one in Foxborough. We'll check them out, grab some dinner, then be back in time for shift change."

Not that it mattered, since everyone was on today and James was staying overnight. But Amelia didn't argue with him. Instead, she said, "Any word from Gabriella and Bradley?"

"Not yet," James said. "I assume we'll hear about how horrible the rest of the family is pretty soon."

Amelia shook her head. "I've never been rich," she said. "But you'd think that no matter how much money you had, you'd be humble enough to let the experts help you when there's literally a curse coming for your family."

"They don't even seem that upset," James said, tearing his gaze away from the blur of trees to face Amelia, whose eyes were on the road. "It's the weirdest thing. They were doing the 'yes, yes, so sad' thing with me and Gabs, but they could have been talking about a flat tire for all the actual sadness they showed. That piece of work over in the hospital was more concerned that the guy who found her was trespassing on their massive woods rather than the fact that he saved her life. And the ones at the summer home thought we were there to steal business secrets."

He shook his head, glancing down as his phone buzzed with an incoming text. It was Gabriella, letting him know they'd arrived at the Cottage, so he responded with a quick thumbs-up before continuing. "So me and Gabs have a massive family. And we don't all get along. But if some horror movie force came in and ripped a couple of my uncles apart, I might have some feelings on the subject, you know? And if there was any chance of it coming for my kids, forget about it. But no, it's all about their stupid clothing store."

"Hell, I have no siblings and no cousins and even I know that," Amelia said, rolling her eyes. "It has to be a money thing."

"Something we're both experts in."

They both laughed at that as Amelia pulled off the highway exit. "Alright, I need you to navigate from here," she said as she merged onto a busy road.

* * *

Ten minutes later, they were pulling up in front of the Delinsky's entrance at an upscale mall tucked way back away from the main road. Christmas shopping was in full swing and the parking lot was a nightmare of cars narrowly missing pedestrians and drivers fighting passive-aggressively over parking spots. Amelia stopped in front of the shop entrance.

"You head in," she said. "I'll go find a spot and meet you."

A car honked behind them, and James grabbed his bag and climbed out. He was barely on the sidewalk before someone cut past the van and took off down the fire lane. Amelia pulled out into a small gap in traffic and James headed inside.

As the door swung shut behind him, James was suddenly completely aware of how worn out his clothes were. The holes in his jeans weren't in trendy spots, and the flannel shirt he wore had a button missing. He zipped his coat, tried to remember he wasn't here to shop, then started walking toward the counter.

Christmas music piped over the speakers, a light, jazzy rendition of "Silver Bells." James still needed to finish his Christmas shopping, but nothing in here was fit for anyone on his Christmas list. One soft wool sweater looked like it might be good for his father, but a quick glance at the price tag changed his mind immediately.

If he spent that much money on a gift for his dad, his dad's gift to him would be a swift kick in the ass, and James knew it. Still, it was a really nice sweater. It almost looked handmade.

The checkout line snaked through velvet ropes as though people were waiting to get into a swanky nightclub. For a second, James hesitated. He'd look like a dick cutting the line, right? But he wasn't shopping, he just needed a manager. So instead, he slipped his Foundation ID out of his wallet and walked over to the side of the line of registers.

"Excuse me," he said to the woman working at the last one.

"Line starts back there, sir," she said without looking at him, beckoning to the next person in line.

"I'm not here to shop. I need to speak to the manager."

"I am the manager," the woman said as she began checking out the stack of dresses the man had brought over. "What can I do for you?"

James glanced at the crowd of people, then back at the manager, who was now bagging the items she'd scanned at an alarming speed. "Is there somewhere we can talk in private?"

Now she turned to him, heavily outlined eyes narrowed in frustration. "Sir, we are extremely busy. Could you possibly come back another time if it's something so personal?"

"It's about the Delinsky family," James said, keeping his voice as low as he dared. "I'm working on behalf of the family, trying to solve the, um, situation that happened this week."

Clearly, the managers had been briefed because she froze, the man's receipt in her hand. Then she sighed and turned to the woman at the next register. "Clara," she said. "I need to take this."

The other woman nodded, and the manager handed the man his receipt. Then she turned off her register light and walked out to James.

"What do you mean you're working for the family?" she asked as she led him further back into the store.

"I mean, I work for the Foundation for Paranormal Studies," James said, handing her his ID to check before she could realize what he'd said and walk away in disgust. "I don't know how much they've told you-"

"They told me my CEO got torn apart on an empty train track and my CFO got decapitated," the manager said, handing back his card. "If they weren't calling that otherworldly, I'd think they were stupider than I already do."

"Not a fan?" James asked as he spotted Amelia walking in.

He motioned her over, and she hurried to catch up with them. "That's my partner," he said as she approached.

"Come into my office," the manager said.

She unlocked an unmarked door and led them into a concrete hallway. While the store was lushly decorated and bright, the only lights here were fluorescent bulbs along the ceiling. They walked halfway down the hall to a room marked OFFICE, which the manager unlocked and guided them into.

It was about the size of James's office and seemed to be used partially for storage. A small desk sat in the corner, along with a couple of folding chairs. The manager motioned toward the chairs, then sat down behind the desk.

"I'm Yolanda," she said.

"James," he said, holding out a hand to shake.

"Amelia."

Once they'd all shook hands and were sitting back down, Yolanda slowly shook her head. "Look," she said. "I can't say I like the Delinsky family, but nobody deserves that."

"Why don't you like them?" James asked.

Yolanda snorted. "You said you're working for them and you can't figure that out?"

"Oh, no, I know my reasoning," James said. "I was just curious about yours."

Yolanda's laugh was warmer this time. "They're good at business, I guess," she said. "But they're not exactly good people."

"Why not?" Amelia asked.

Yolanda sighed. "They only care about profits," she said. "Business has been slowing down some over the past year and they ended up cutting benefits and laying people off. It happened in waves, but we lost a lot of people who had worked here for years."

"Shit," James murmured.

"Yeah," Yolanda said, absently fiddling with a pen cap on her desk. "And then they send us these newsletters that include pictures of the Thanksgiving parties they're hosting over at The Cottage at Delinsky Cove, as they keep calling it. They're these lavish things and they don't seem to realize or care that they're sending these to staffers who are working overtime and fearing layoffs."

Based on what he'd seen yesterday at said Cottage, James wasn't all that surprised, though a frisson of disgust went through him. This was a little too close to home, wasn't it? But at least the Foundation had promised no layoffs with all their blustering about belt-tightening. Clearly making the same connection, Amelia stole a glance at him.

"Do you think someone in the company was involved?" Yolanda asked.

"No idea," James said quickly. "We're gathering all the information we can and looking into all possibilities."

"We have a good crew here," Yolanda said. "I can't imagine anyone here doing something like this."

"I'm sure," Amelia said. "You know them best."

"Is there anything else I can help you with?" Yolanda asked. "I'm sorry to rush you, it's just that, you know, Christmas and we're short-staffed."

"Oh, right," James said, hurriedly standing up. "No, I think that's it for now. Thank you so much for your time."

Chapter 9

It was bright and sunny as they walked out of the store, but the sharp chill in the air went straight through James's unzipped jacket. "What do you think?" Amelia asked as they started across the parking lot.

"I think I've seen people do worse for less," James muttered, yanking up the zipper on his coat.

Amelia was silent, and James almost regretted bringing it up. But as they got into the car, she said, "Revenge is a good motive. But are we thinking there's someone with this kind of ability working for minimum wage at a clothing store? If I could kill people with magic, I wouldn't be working in customer service."

She took out her phone and called Headquarters. A second later, Graham picked up.

"Any leads?" he asked.

"Maybe?" Amelia said. "Apparently, the Delinskys have really screwed their employees lately and are either completely oblivious to how it looks, or they're rubbing it in."

She put her phone in the holder mounted on their dashboard and turned on the van. It hesitated for a moment, then rumbled to life. "We've got another location we're going to look at in a little while. If we get similar answers there, we'll need to look more into how someone could do this and get away with it."

"The methods of death are so violent and out there," Madelyn said from slightly off-speaker. "And didn't Rita Delinsky say she was transported from outside Boston?"

"Same with the others," Amelia said. "So either it teleported them or mind-controlled them into traveling out here to die."

"That's some intense power," James said, his heart sinking a little.

His own deep terror of mind control aside, this kind of investigation was outside of what they normally dealt with. While the magic was pretty typical, something this powerful with a full investigation, including this many moving parts, was different.

"We might need to try and bring in a curse expert," he said as Amelia slowly drove out of the parking lot. "Hopefully, the Foundation has someone that can help."

"Bradley just called in from Ashburnham," Madelyn said, closer to the speaker now. "They met with more family members today. No real new information, but he said he doesn't think it's from the family. They're awful, but they're awful together."

"No signs of any estranged family members?" James asked.

"Not that they could tell," Madelyn replied. "He said they asked, but they were tripping over themselves to assure him and Gabriella that nobody in the family would ever risk that."

"Risk leaving or risk killing them?"

"Both, I guess?"

"We're heading over to the next location now," James said, pulling up the map on his own phone. "It's about twenty-five minutes from here. We'll probably grab a quick supper while we're out, then head back to headquarters. Text me if you want us to pick you up anything."

They hung up a second later, just as Amelia was pulling onto the highway. James pulled out his phone to see a text from Gabriella.

GABRIELLA

It's not the family. They're awful, but they're all invested.

He typed out his reply.

JAMES

In the business or in each other?

GABRIELLA

The business. These people don't give a shit about each other.

"Gabs is saying the same thing," James told Amelia as she passed a tractor-trailer, then moved back into the middle lane.

"So that narrows the possible suspects down to, oh, twenty shops?" Amelia said. "Not to mention the friends and family we haven't found yet who might want revenge."

"If the Foundation wants us doing full investigations, they better start acting like it," James said, rolling his eyes as he scanned through his email.

There was one from McGovern, thanking him for sending the reports and asking for updates on this case. This was, again, shockingly reasonable. Despite his irritation at the Foundation in general, James sent a quick reply, then put the map back up on his screen and put it on the dashboard mount.

He had twenty-five minutes to mull this all over before they reached their next stop.

* * *

The next shop was in an equally upscale, equally cut-throat mall. Again, Amelia dropped James at the front door like she was dropping her kid off at school, then weaved her way through the crowds to find a parking space as he went inside.

This Delinsky's location was almost identical to the first one. Christmas greenery in every corner and draped tastefully over displays, warm gold fixtures polished to perfection, and smooth jazz carols drifting on the lightly scented air. James tensed up immediately as he walked inside.

Again, he made his way up to the busy checkout counter. "Excuse me," he said to the man at the end register.

"Busy," the man snapped, "Please come back later."

He was a tall man, probably a little taller than James, and maybe a little older. But there was an unhealthy look to him, a pinched, sallow vibe that immediately caught James's attention. "I need to speak to a manager," he said. "It's a work matter."

"She's gone," the man said, still not looking at him as he scanned the pile of scarves in front of him.

"Is there someone else?"

"No."

"Who's in charge?"

Frustration was bubbling in James's chest, but getting belligerent wouldn't help. Not when he could almost see the steam coming from this guy's ears already. The guy finally turned to him. "It's Gary," he snapped. "But he's not here right now."

James glanced at the other register, where a young woman was standing completely still, clearly listening to the whole interaction. She barely seemed to notice the customer in front of her until they talked to her, causing her to jump and rush to serve them.

Odd.

"Look," James said. "I'm an investigator working on behalf of the Delinsky family and I really need to speak to your manager. Do you know when he'll be in?"

"No idea," the man said. "If you're really an investigator, you'll need to figure it out yourself. Next customer."

He motioned for the person at the front of the line, deliberately turning his body away from James. This wasn't worth arguing about right now. He'd just come back.

He ran a hand through his hair and sighed, glancing down at the man's name tag. "Fine," he said. "Thanks for your help, um, Jeremy."

The man's eyes narrowed, but he still didn't turn back to James. James turned and walked away, reaching the front door as Amelia was coming in.

"Don't bother," he said. "We need to come back later."

Amelia looked curiously behind him toward the register, but followed him out without argument. "What was that about?" she asked as they crossed the street into the densely packed parking lot.

"Manager apparently isn't on today and the guy at the register was not feeling chatty," James replied. "He was aggressive about it."

"I mean, they were clearly busy."

"Yeah, but still. Whatever. He said to call and find out when the manager was in because he didn't know. Or, wait…"

He paused as he pulled open the passenger side door and climbed into the van. "He said there was no manager, but this guy Gary was in charge and wasn't there. Whatever that means."

"I guess we'll have to ask Gary."

"Yeah."

Amelia carefully eased the van out of the tiny parking spot. "By the way, do you want me to drive?" James asked. "You've been driving all day."

"Nah," she said. "I'm already going. But you can drive home if you really want to."

"Always."

She laughed. "Alright, I'm hungry," she said, heading toward the parking lot exit. "Where are we getting lunch?"

* * *

They stopped for burritos at a small place off the highway, about ten minutes away from the mall. After texting the others, they got orders for everyone, stacking the brown paper bags on the table as they sat down to eat their own food. It was a fairly long drive home, maybe an hour or so, but it wasn't like anyone was going to complain if their food was cold.

James ate his burrito quickly, sitting at the tiny table inside the restaurant with Amelia. She'd gotten some kind of burrito salad or something, and she mixed it all together as she sat down.

"So Gabriella mentioned some guy named Zach?" Amelia asked.

James took a sip of his Diet Coke and nodded. "Yeah," he said. "I guess he's the nephew or something. Seems like a decent guy, despite being a Delinsky."

"That's what she said," Amelia said. "He was one of the ones they interviewed today and was one of two Delinskys to show any hint of emotion."

"Hmm."

He took a bite of his burrito and realized far too late that he recognized that look in her eye. "She also said he was flirting with you yesterday."

James held up a finger, swallowed his food, and took another sip of his drink. "No," he said finally. "He handed me a business card and said to let him know if we needed anything."

"But was it like, you needed anything or you *needed* anything?"

James rolled his eyes. "Gabriella has too much time on her hands, apparently," he said. "He wasn't flirting."

Amelia shrugged. "Okay, I believe you."

She clearly didn't. "Good."

"Bradley said he's a dick."

"High praise from a true expert in the field."

"Maybe if you got laid once in a while-"

He held up a hand to stop her. This was not what they were discussing over lunch, not even if it was just the two of them. "Listen," he said. "Even if he was flirting, I'm not dating someone involved in the case. I'm not that unprofessional."

Amelia shrugged. "Sure thing. Let's finish up and get on the road before the traffic gets bad."

James waited cautiously to see if she really was going to let it go. She didn't say another word as she picked up the bags of takeout, but the slight smirk never left her face.

* * *

Five minutes later, they were back in the van, and James was pulling out of the tiny parking lot. "Looks like snow," he said, glancing up at the sky.

The clouds were hanging heavier above them than they had before, even though they hadn't stopped for very long. He couldn't see any flakes yet, but suddenly had the urge to get home as fast as possible to avoid driving in it.

"The weather can't decide what it wants to be today," Amelia said, shaking her head. "Alright, you know where you're going, right?"

He nodded, pulling out into the stream of traffic passing by the restaurant. "Yeah, it's nothing," he said.

The sun was already going down, so they were likely to hit traffic on the way home, especially since they were fairly close to the city. But it wasn't quite as late as it felt. James hated that about December. It got so dark so early, it felt like it was so much later than it really was.

"So Chris is moving," he said as he drove through an intersection heading away from the business district and into a more wooded patch of road. "He's going into the woods to find himself or something. So now we need a new roommate."

"Got anyone in mind?" Amelia asked.

"Not yet," James replied, frowning as the van bucked slightly. "Hey, did you notice anything weird with the van while you were driving?"

"No," she said. "It seemed fine to me."

He tested the gas pedal, and it seemed smooth. Maybe it was the engine? They'd have to throw repairs on the list of expenses in that case. Shit, he could hear Bradley's complaints already. The van was in for repairs at least three times a year, usually more. And it had been the branch's official vehicle for as long as James had worked there.

As much sentimental feeling as he might have held for it, this was getting ridiculous. When was it going to be worth scrapping the van and getting something new? Probably never, if the Foundation had anything to say about it.

"I'll take a look when we get back," James said. "It's probably just the cold or something."

He tried the brake, and it easily lowered under his foot as the van slowed down. Yeah, this was fine. It was just the van acting up. And as a knocking noise appeared from somewhere in the rear, he glanced at the GPS to see that they had another forty minutes at least.

"Chris said he'll help, but me and Graham are both a little uneasy about that," he continued, trying to push the strange, expensive-sounding problem out of his mind. "We'll probably end up with his brother or something."

Amelia laughed. "Hey, at least he paid his rent. It could be worse."

"Yeah, true."

"Have you considered putting up a notice online? That's how you got Chris in the first place, right?"

James went to answer, but then there was another sputter and the van jolted forward, throwing them both in their seats. James's seatbelt bit into his waist and he grunted in pain. "Shit," he said. "Hopefully it's just the cold."

It was well above freezing, but neither of them said anything about it. Instead, they were silent as the van rolled toward the highway. It was fine, it was just an old vehicle acting up, nothing to worry about.

They reached the top of the sloping hill and James tapped the brake to slow down as they descended. This time, the pedal collapsed under his foot and the van's speed didn't change.

Fuck. He tapped the brake again, praying he'd just done it wrong somehow the first time. But again, it sank too loosely, the pedal mushy under his foot. The van continued to speed up as it rolled down the empty street, passing a small house before they were surrounded by trees.

"What's going on?" Amelia demanded.

"The brakes aren't working," James replied, desperately hitting the pedal again.

"What do you mean, they aren't working?"

Amelia's voice was rising and nausea rose in James's panicked throat as the van moved faster and faster down the hill. There was still no one around, but there were curves in the road ahead and if they were moving this fast or faster, they could hit another car or go off the road, or...

He tried to remember what he'd learned in drivers' education years earlier, but they didn't go over this, did they? The worst thing they focused on was parallel parking, and he still sucked at that. James hoped they'd reach the bottom of the hill soon and coast to a stop, but a glance at the steep drops full of trees on each side of the road showed that wasn't likely to happen.

The van was going so fast that the trees were blurring together. The brakes were completely gone as he tried over and over again to get them to engage. All thought had left James's brain except FIX IT! Could he turn to the side and slow down the momentum? Or what? Was there anything he could do?

"TURN!" Amelia screamed.

There was a sharp turn in the road ahead, and James wrenched the steering wheel to the side. The van skidded on the road, which was thankfully empty in the opposite lane. He tried to get the van going straight, but it was tipping too far to the side, two tires completely off the road now.

And then it was on its side, then rolling, tossing the two of them painfully despite their seatbelts. James's head whipped forward, then backward, and he heard the sound of Amelia's head making contact with something as the van rolled.

Then the road dropped away sickeningly below them and sparks flew past the closed window as they went through the guardrail. As the van slid down the side of the embankment, James knew they weren't getting out of this.

Chapter 10

There was a horn blaring somewhere far away. Whoever that was needed to shut up. No one cared. James tried to get up and yell at them to turn it off, knock it off, no one needs that right now.

"Sir?"

A light hand on his shoulder and James remembered everything. He sat up painfully, lifting his head from the steering wheel. The horn stopped abruptly.

"Sir, it's okay," a young woman was saying. "You've been in an accident. We're here to help."

He turned to see that the seat next to him was empty. Panic cut through the fog in his brain. "Where's Amelia?" he demanded.

"Your friend is in the ambulance," the woman replied. "Come on, we need to get you out of here."

She reached over him and tried to unbuckle his seatbelt. It was jammed, so after a moment, she just sliced it apart and reached for his hand. James shakily got out of the seat, relieved that nothing seemed to be broken.

"You need to go to the hospital," the woman said.

"No, I'm fine. Did someone check Robin?"

"Who's Robin? Was there someone else in the car? I only saw two adults in the front seat."

Wait, which car accident was this? James shook his head. "I'm sorry," he said. "No, it was just the two of us."

"Let's get up to the road so we can check you out. It's okay, it's probably just shock."

Another paramedic was there now, a large, silent man. Between the two of them, they helped James up to the top of the embankment. The guardrail was smashed where the van had gone off the road and he could see an ambulance hurrying away.

"I need you to walk nine steps, heel to toe, along the white line."

The male paramedic's voice was gruff and James followed the instructions without thinking, the world still spinning slightly around him as he walked along the side of the road. He knew his balance was off and he staggered, a bolt of pain going through his head before he'd even made it to the third step. He dropped to his knees before reaching a fourth.

The man's voice was above him now. "Stand up, get on one leg."

Was he hallucinating? James stood up straight, but even before one foot was fully off the ground, he was falling again. The female paramedic caught him and he heard her say something to the man.

"We need to give you a blood alcohol test," the man said. "Were you drinking tonight?"

It took a moment for the words to penetrate as James looked around the darkening wooded road, the lights on the police cruiser and ambulance pulsing hypnotically beside them. He turned to the man, who he now realized was a cop. "I'm not drunk," he said.

"Can you tell us what happened?" the cop asked, sounding almost disinterested as he pulled out the breathalyzer.

"The... the brakes failed," he said. "We were on our way home and they stopped working."

"Blow."

Mortified tears pricked his eyes as he leaned in and blew into the tube, sending another spike of pain through his head. "We were working," he said.

"Witness back there said they saw you zigzagging on the road," the cop said.

"It's my brakes," James repeated, trying to stay calm.

The paramedic put a hand on his shoulder. A moment later, the cop looked at the test and grunted. "You're fine," he said.

"I'm taking him to the hospital, that's a non-existent blood alcohol content," the paramedic said. "Come on. Don't worry, hon, she'll be okay."

James wanted to get his stuff. His wallet was in the car and he should probably care about the Foundation gear in the backseat. But when he glanced down the hill and saw the smoking wreck of the van jammed between two trees, he nearly threw up. Stomach cold and mouth flooding with the taste of bile, he followed the paramedic to the ambulance.

Things got a little fuzzy as they were heading to the hospital. The paramedic was taking his vitals and talking to him, but it was as though all the energy had left his body and all he had left in him was worry. He didn't know how much later it was, but eventually, he was in a hospital emergency room, tucked away in an alcove where nobody was able to tell him anything about Amelia.

He needed to get a phone. His own phone was smashed up in the van, along with his bag and ID. He needed to let the rest of the team know they were there. Graham and Madelyn were probably trying to get in touch with them right now. Did Amelia have her phone? Was she even conscious?

A young doctor came in a few minutes later to examine him. After a few minutes of uncomfortable inspection, she said that it seemed to be mostly bumps and bruises, probably some whiplash, but they'd do a scan for concussion. Any relief he felt from this was fleeting as he looked up at her from the bed.

"What about Amelia?" he asked.

"Who's that?"

"My friend. She was in the car with me. They said she got taken here too."

"She's probably still getting checked," the doctor said with an attempt at a comforting smile. "Just relax. She's in good hands."

He waited alone for an excruciating half-hour after that. A nurse came in eventually and set him up with an IV and some pain medication. It dulled the physical pain a little, letting him concentrate more on the fear that was churning inside him.

How long has he been here? He needed to get in touch with Headquarters.

"Excuse me," he said, next time the same nurse came into his alcove. "Is there a phone I could use? Mine's missing and I really need to tell my work where we are."

"Hang on," the nurse said. "I'll check for you."

She walked out, sliding the door halfway shut behind her. James sat back against the bed and tried to relax. The searing burn where his seatbelt had cut into his torso was ebbing now, along with the pain in his head and neck, thanks to the medication. He glanced at the IV tube snaking into the port in his arm, then sighed.

There was nothing he could do. But he'd been the one driving, and he needed to make sure Amelia was okay.

Had he caused it? He hadn't been drinking, but maybe that didn't matter. Maybe he'd fucked up somewhere along the line today and broken the van. No, they should have fought for a new one earlier. If he'd been more adamant about it, maybe the Foundation would have listened.

The nurse popped her head back in. "Give me just a second," she said. "There's something going on at the nurse's station and then I'll see what I can do for you."

She hurried back out and James heard someone down the hall say, "Sir, you can't be in here unless you're with a patient."

"I'm here for two of them," a familiar voice snapped. "Ask Deb out at reception, she'll vouch for me."

Now he had to be hallucinating. It was the pain meds, they were stronger than he thought. James pushed himself up and carefully unraveled the IV pole from the tangle of equipment behind the bed. He stood up carefully, briefly wondered where his shoes were, then stepped out of the alcove, gripping the IV pole as it rolled beside him.

No, he was right. Bradley was standing at the nurse's station, holding his ID out to the charge nurse with a shaking hand. James stepped out a little farther.

"Brad," he called, cringing at how weak his voice sounded.

He cleared his throat and went to try again. But before he could, Bradley spun in his direction, as did every nurse surrounding them. James nodded, wobbling slightly as he waved to the nurses. "He's with me. Sorry."

Bradley looked more irritated than relieved and if James hadn't known him for years, he would have thought that really was the case. He walked toward

James, who was clinging to the IV pole for dear life. As he got to the alcove doorway, James, in a moment of fear, painkiller haze, or both, threw his arms around Bradley's neck. Bradley's coat was cold under his chin and he realized his fuckup immediately as Bradley froze in his grip. But then, shockingly, his arms were around James too.

"You idiot," Bradley snapped, still gripping him tightly. "Get back in the bed before you kill yourself."

The first nurse was back now, and she helped James back onto the bed, telling him if he needed to get up again, to call her or let his friend help. He nodded and then she walked out, leaving them alone.

"They won't tell me where Amelia is," James said. "They keep telling me she's probably fine, but no one has any actual information."

"I'll find out," Bradley said. "Madelyn is here too, she's out in the waiting room. Hang on, I'll be right back."

He slipped out of the room, and James closed his eyes for a moment. The fear wasn't gone, but at least there were a couple more people here to help with it. That was, if Bradley didn't get himself thrown out of the emergency room.

Before Bradley got back, a tech arrived to wheel James away for a CT scan. After what felt like forever, but was probably only twenty minutes or so, he was back in his alcove, where Bradley was waiting.

"How did you know we were here?" James asked, reaching for a cup of water on the small table beside him.

"They called us," Bradley replied. "Amelia's Foundation ID had us listed as her emergency contact."

"They didn't do that for me."

"That's because you never sent in that paperwork," Bradley retorted, rolling his eyes.

"How is she?" James asked.

"She's okay," Bradley replied, and a wave of relief crashed over James. "They said she'll probably be admitted overnight. I saw her a few minutes ago. She's out of it, but okay. Broken arm, I think."

The mix of relief and shame took his breath away. "I don't know what happened," James said. "The brakes stopped working. I don't know if it's something I did."

"Like what?" Bradley asked, looking up at the equipment piled in the corner of the alcove.

"I don't know. But the van just stopped working," James said. "It was fine the whole time. Then we were on our way back and the brakes just stopped working."

"Like they'd been cut?"

James thought of the squishy sensation of the pedal under his foot. "Yeah."

"And you were at Delinsky's before that."

"Are you saying-"

"I'm not saying anything," Bradley said, waving a hand. "That'd be irresponsible."

Shit, he didn't need to because now James was putting all the pieces together himself. "We went to Delinsky's before lunch," he said, lowering his voice. "The man I spoke to there said that they had no manager. He was really aggressive about getting me the hell out of there."

"Huh."

Bradley didn't say anything else after that, and James was too exhausted to do more than worry about it.

Chapter 11

A little while later, James walked slowly out into the ER waiting room, his whole body aching despite the painkillers in his system. Madelyn was sitting in a seat near the front entrance and as soon as she saw him, she stood up and hurried over as quickly as she could on her cane.

"I was so worried," she said, wrapping her arms around him.

He squeezed her carefully, then they both sat back down in the uncomfortable chairs. "Amelia's here for a while longer," Madelyn said. "I don't know if she's being admitted or not, so I'm going to stay. Bradley's going to drive back with you."

Most days, James would rather take his chances driving the van back. But all he wanted right now was to be in bed, whether at home or at Headquarters. So he nodded and sat with her for a moment. After a few minutes, the doors slid open to the entrance and Bradley walked in. He spotted them and walked over.

"My car is outside," he said. "Are you ready?"

Maybe not for a walk to the car, but James could suck it up for a moment. Madelyn squeezed his hand, and he stood up. "Keep us updated," he said.

She nodded. James followed after Bradley, who was walking too quickly toward his car. It ended up being parked right outside, hazard lights flashing. Relieved, James slid into the passenger seat. "Thanks," he said.

Bradley shrugged and pulled out of the fire lane. James gingerly pulled on his seatbelt, trying fruitlessly to keep it from rubbing against the gauze over his previous seatbelt injuries. They drove in silence for a while, James gazing out into the darkness. He had no idea what time it was or what town they were in. Hell, he didn't even recognize the name of the hospital as they drove away.

"Graham and Gabriella are still at Headquarters," Bradley said, stopping at a red light just outside of the hospital parking lot. "I'm going to take over once we get there, since you and Amelia are both injured and Madelyn is staying here. Do you want me to drop you off at home?"

"No, I'll go to Headquarters."

Bradley raised an eyebrow, still looking at the road. "You sure?"

"Yeah, I can't deal with our other roommate right now."

"Fine. I need to stop by my house after, though."

"You can go while I'm here. No point in going out again after we get back."

Bradley didn't say anything, but his mouth was a thin line. It was the first slight bit of normalcy tonight, and James would take it. So instead of continuing to argue, he turned back to the sky.

Amelia was going to be okay. He was okay. The van was wrecked, but they'd figure that part out. And the accident had happened out of nowhere after an encounter with someone who didn't want to talk to them.

"If you wanted to use magic to kill someone, how would you do it?" James asked, trying vaguely to remember his celestial navigation training as he looked up at the stars.

"In a way that looks like a complete accident," Bradley replied without hesitation.

James looked at him. "You've thought about that before, haven't you?"

Bradley shrugged and kept driving. "The Delinsky deaths were so... grotesque," James continued. "And Rita Delinsky survived, but hers would have been weird too if that guy hadn't found her out on the ice."

"Do you think the same person that tried to kill you killed them?"

"Yeah."

Bradley nodded. "Well, they fucked it up."

"Which maybe means they were sloppy," James said, resting his head against the back of the seat. "Because they were in a hurry. I think it was that guy at the Delinsky's shop. And he probably did the rest of it, too."

"How?" Bradley asked. "That's serious magic."

"I don't know."

He expected a comment on his intellect, but there was nothing.

"By the way," Bradley said after a few minutes of silence. "I heard about your plans to specialize the team. Hire an ambulance driver. I'm sick of bringing people to and from the hospital."

James rolled his eyes, but he could tell there was no fire behind the complaint. "I'll make you an official hospital liaison," he said. "Get you a shiny quarter for a raise since the generosity of the Foundation knows no bounds."

Maybe it was the dark or the drugs, but he could have sworn he saw Bradley laugh at that.

* * *

An hour later, they were passing through Leominster, skipping the exit James always took back to Headquarters. Once they were in Fitchburg a few minutes later, James was surprised when they pulled up outside of a small, old apartment building. Bradley turned off the car and got out. James followed, moving slowly.

"Oh," Bradley said, as James closed his door. "I didn't think you were coming."

"Do you not want me to?"

"I don't care."

There were probably four or five units in this building, but only two other cars in the small lot directly outside of it. James followed Bradley into the depressing front hall, then stepped back as Bradley unlocked the door. "I'm on the first floor," he said.

The halls were harshly lit with the same fluorescent lights James had seen in the space behind Delinsky's earlier that day. The part they were in was short, with only two units at the end. It looked a lot like the places where

James had lived before his current apartment, which wasn't any fancier. But Bradley looked apprehensive, like he was waiting for a comment.

He unlocked the door to the first unit and stepped in. "Look out for the cat," he said.

"You have a cat?"

"No, my roommates do."

If it weren't for the dull throbbing in his head, James would think this was a dream. There was no way he was actually standing in his prickly teammate's home right now. But he was, and it was a dingy-looking place. The living room they were in was clean, but the walls were gloomy despite the concert posters and framed paintings on the walls. Beyond it was a small kitchenette and a long, dark hallway that must have led toward the bedrooms.

"Right back," Bradley said, disappearing down the hall.

James stood awkwardly in the living room, looking around. A couch and a large TV took up most of the back half of the room, then there was a small card table. From here, he could see into the kitchenette, which was crammed with cooking equipment and a sink overflowing with dishes.

"How many roommates do you have?" he asked as Bradley came back down the hall with a bag in his hand.

"Two, why?"

"Geez, just asking."

Bradley still looked a little defensive, but just shrugged. "They're a couple," he said. "They're young and they like to have parties here. Somehow. They're fine."

James couldn't even begin to imagine how a party would work in this apartment, but it didn't matter because they were leaving and he'd probably never be back here again. He followed Bradley out into the bright hallway again, then waited as Bradley locked the door. "Are you sure you want to go to headquarters?" Bradley asked again.

"Yeah," James said. "I'm on tonight, anyway."

Bradley raised an eyebrow and James didn't need him to say a word to get his frustration across. "Fine, I won't work," he said. "But I still would rather go there than home. Otherwise, I'll just be mad at our housemate and worried about Amelia."

"Your choice," Bradley said, hurrying toward the front door.

About fifteen minutes later, they were pulling into the driveway at Headquarters. As Bradley killed the car engine, James cleared his throat.

"Um, thanks for picking me up," he said.

"It's not like the van was getting you home," Bradley said, turning to grab his bag out of the backseat.

"I know," James said, wondering why he had expected anything more than that. "But still."

"Yeah, sure."

Bradley got out of the car and James followed, his whole body aching. As he walked inside, he heard Gabriella hurrying over to them. She moved to give him a hug, then paused.

"Are you okay?" she asked.

He nodded, then reached over to hug her instead. She, too, squeezed him gently, then moved aside as he slowly walked up the stairs.

"I'm fine," he said. "I just need some sleep."

"Madelyn just called a minute ago," Gabriella said. "They're admitting Amelia for the night for observation. She's going to drive back here, then go get Amelia tomorrow."

"Is she feeling up to it?" James asked.

"Seems to be," Gabriella replied. "She said worst case, her stepmother's house is along the way and she can spend the night there."

"Good."

Graham walked over from the comms and gave James a gentle clap on the shoulder. "Glad you're okay, man," he said. "We were really scared."

James laughed wearily. "Me too."

He was close to falling down now that the adrenaline was long gone. "I'll be in the gray bedroom," he said. "Wake me up if you need me."

They all nodded, though he knew no one would. But instead of trying to insist, he turned and trudged down the hall to the bedroom. His overnight bag was still sitting on the bed where he'd dropped it this morning. He shoved it aside, then climbed under the covers, falling asleep in seconds.

He woke up from dreams of approaching Robin's smoking car about an hour later, heart racing. But it hadn't been fully Robin's car. It had been the van, too. And yet again, someone had been trying to kill him in it. Just like in real life.

He kind of wanted to consider that a little deeper, but he fell back to sleep before he could.

Chapter 12

James woke up to someone shaking his shoulder, the sensation dragging him up through quicksand. He lifted his head off the pillow and squinted at the intruder. "Hmm?"

"Hey man," Graham said in a half-whisper. "Sorry, but Chris just called. He's got a prospective roommate lined up that he wants us to meet today."

Today? James realized the light coming in the windows wasn't as thin as it normally was when he woke up in this room. "What time is it?" he asked, sitting up.

"Eleven."

"What?"

He quickly sat up all the way, then fell back down as his body protested the movement. His joints felt stiff and sore and the places on his torso where the seat belt had dug into his flesh burned. His head hit the pillow, and he groaned as his neck protested.

"Yeah, don't worry about it," Graham said. "I just got here a little while ago. Bradley and Madelyn have been trading off leadership duties and so far, the apocalypse has skipped over Leominster."

"Maybe if I stay in bed a little longer," James muttered.

"Chris wants the guy to come over at six," Graham said. "Are you here then?"

"No idea," James said. "Let me think."

He took a beat to try to clear the cobwebs a little. "Um, yeah," he said. "Wait, no. I was supposed to do the overnight last night and the day shift today. It's eleven?"

"You're injured. No one was going to mess with you," Graham said. "I'm home at five, so we can both be there."

"Thank God," James muttered.

He slowly sat up again, bracing himself on the bed as he moved. Nothing seemed to be broken that hadn't been yesterday. Instead, he just felt sore and grumpy. Coffee and Tylenol would help with that as much as anything would.

"Amelia called from the hospital," Graham said. "She's doing well."

"I'm so glad. Sorry, I should have talked to her."

"Yeah, she said don't worry about it. She didn't want to wake you up. But they're going to release her later today and Madelyn's picking her up."

James wanted to ask if Madelyn was okay with the trip, but he knew that would be pushing it. If she wanted to get Amelia and felt up for the drive, he'd just appreciate it. And be available if she changed her mind.

"Is Madelyn here now?" he asked.

"Yeah, everybody is except Bradley. He took your shift last night, so we forced him to go home for a while."

James would have to thank him later, even if he got a snarling response. He stood up and shook his head slightly, trying and failing to clear it. "I'm going to shower and have some coffee, then I can come join you guys," he said.

"Don't hurry," Graham said. "You shouldn't be working. You probably shouldn't even be here."

"You want to be home solo with a Chris who's finding himself?" James asked.

"No," Graham admitted. "Fair. But you're not working more than a little today. If I can't stop you, Madelyn is going to."

"And my injuries are two years old, so you can't use them as an excuse."

James jumped as Madelyn's voice came from the open door. She walked into the room with a smile. "How are you?" she asked.

"Sore," he admitted with a laugh. "And I apparently slept twelve hours."

"You can't count that as your vacation," she said. "We're taking today off from the Delinsky case. Father McEnerney called earlier, horrified about what happened. He's coming tomorrow to give you and Amelia some extra protection and reinforce some things around the house. If the Foundation even attempts to give you a hard time about it, I have a feeling they'll be dealing with him."

Father McEnerney seemed harmless, but James had worked with him long enough to know otherwise. And he could use a quiet day. Not that he was going to completely ignore work, but the idea of driving anywhere made him queasy. So rather than argue, he nodded.

"I'm going to shower," he said again. "Then I'll be out to sit on the couch or something."

Neither of the others seemed to find anything wrong with this, so he walked out of the room and made his way to the bathroom. Before he got there, Gabriella was hurrying down the hall toward him.

"Your mom wants you to call her."

Oh fuck. "I will," James said. "I'm just going to shower first."

"She said your phone is disconnected, so she called my mom, who called me."

"It broke in the crash," James said. "Did you tell her I was fine?"

"I did," Gabriella said. "And I told your dad, too. And Uncle Tommy."

"Uncle Tommy called?"

Gabriella seemed as perplexed by this as he did. "Yeah, he called my phone. I didn't even know he had my number. He was concerned it was paranormal."

"I mean, it was," James muttered. "We just need to prove it. But for real, I need to shower, then I'll call my mom."

* * *

Half an hour later, James was getting off of the most guilt-inducing call he'd ever made. His mom wasn't doing it on purpose. It wasn't even her fault. But between the sobs when she picked up the call and the offers to buy him a new phone, to bring him soup, to do anything he needed, he was heartbroken he'd scared her like that. Then his father had gotten on the line and it had been more of the same, his usually stoic father offering any help he could with a shake in his voice that James never wanted to hear again.

He finally hung up, then set the phone back in the cradle with a sigh. He'd been awake less than an hour and already wanted to go back to bed. But before he could do anything, Gabriella walked into the room, her own phone to her ear.

"Yeah, hang on,"

She took the phone down, muffling the speaker in her hand. "It's Uncle Tommy," she said. "He wants to talk to you."

They exchanged baffled glances, then James took the phone. "Hey, Uncle Tommy."

"Hey, kid, how are you doing?"

Their uncle's voice was still booming over the phone, even as he clearly tried to contain it. "I'm fine," James said. "Just sore."

"Yeah, that's a real sonofabitch thing to have happened. On Foundation business?"

"Yeah, in the official vehicle."

"What's the case?"

He wasn't allowed to go into detail, but it wasn't like Uncle Tommy was going to call the press. "I think it's a curse," he said. "We're still sorting it out."

"That's what I figured. But listen, kid, if you need, I got some buddies who are pretty good at this kind of thing. Just in case there's anything that slips through the cracks with the Foundation, you know?"

Uncle Tommy, while not a professional, had his own experience with the paranormal. Back when James had been about twenty, Uncle Tommy had encountered vampires on a camping trip out in the small town of Savoy. James didn't know the details, but he did know that while the Foundation had been involved in the investigation, Uncle Tommy and Aunt Mary had been the ones to get it all under control. So if Uncle Tommy was offering help, James knew it was legit.

Potentially not legal, but legit.

"Thanks," he said. "Um, yeah, I'll see what happens from here, but I'll keep it in mind."

"Yeah, I got my buddy Eric, up in New Hampshire. He's got a house full of this shit. So just let me know."

They chatted another minute, then James begged off the phone. After a few more minutes of trying to end the conversation, they finally hung up, and he handed Gabriella back her phone. "He's got a buddy who can help us," he said as she slid it into her pocket.

"Do you think it's legitimate?"

"He says so. But we need to figure out what the hell we're dealing with before we can even begin to get rid of it. But I'm almost positive it's a curse."

The side of his head where he'd been talking to Uncle Tommy was ringing. He knew the others were right, he shouldn't be here. But maybe if he just sat on the couch and never moved again, he'd feel better soon.

Chapter 13

"It all fits," Gabriella said, sitting down next to James on the couch a few minutes later. "The timing, the curse, it makes sense. But, um, do you have, like, lost time or anything?"

James frowned. "What do you mean?"

"Is there any point before the accident that you don't remember?"

"No?"

"Amelia said the same thing."

"Gabs, I wasn't drinking."

Gabriella looked at him in alarm. "What the hell? No, of course not. Jesus, James, I was talking about mind control. Who the hell would think you were drunk?"

"The cop that found us. Mind control?"

"It isn't that far out there if it's connected to the Delinskys, remember?" Gabriella said. "Something made Rita Delinsky travel from Wellesley to Ashburnham without even knowing it."

"No, I don't have any points I don't remember," James said. "And I was with Amelia the whole time. So I don't think anything made either of us cut our own brakes."

"So either it's a different curse or it was quick and sloppy."

James rubbed his forehead, trying to shake the queasy feeling that even the mention of mind control gave him. "Apparently. If we're thinking of a curse. Which I am, but we need more information about pretty much everything first."

"Who do we need to talk to?" Gabriella asked.

James thought for a second. "Um, we need more information about what happened to the dead Delinskys. Rita Delinsky, I guess. That jackass at the Foxborough location."

"Bradley sent in a request to the Foundation for all the information they have on the dead Delinskys before he left," Gabriella said. "I'm keeping an eye out for that to come in."

Her next words were interrupted by the phone ringing again. Gabriella picked it up. "North County, Gabriella speaking."

She paused and James could hear someone on the other end, just barely. "Yeah, hang on, he's right here."

She handed the phone to James. "Liaison," she whispered.

James cringed, then held the phone to his ear. "James here."

"James!"

McGovern's voice was loud against his pounding head, and James resisted the urge to once again pull away from the receiver. Where had these people learned to talk on the phone? "Yeah."

"How are you feeling? I received the report of everything that happened last night."

"Not bad," he said. "I don't know what kind of shape the van is in, but we're both alright."

"Good, good," McGovern said. "Don't worry about the van, we'll figure it out."

"Oh, um, thanks," James said.

"We'll get it to one of our partner garages and it'll be good as new," McGovern continued.

There was the delusional Foundation optimism James had been expecting. He hadn't seen the full damage to the van yet, but there had certainly been smoke and crushed steel as he'd gotten out of it.

"I'll need you to file an official report," McGovern said. "Bradley sent one in, but since he's not the captain or second in command, it can't be official."

"Fine," James said.

He'd just copy Bradley's and change a few words. "Is there anything else?"

"Just that the Delinsky family sends their regards," McGovern said. "You can resume your investigations tomorrow."

Father McEnerney must have gotten to them, James thought. "Thank you," he said out loud. "I'll be here at Headquarters today, but it won't be a full workday. Amelia is being released from the hospital and I'm on rest orders."

"Of course," McGovern said. "We don't want to impede that. I'll check in later."

"Thanks."

McGovern hung up and James reluctantly stood to put the phone back on the cradle. Seconds after he'd sat back down, it rang again.

"Motherfucker..." James muttered as he stood up, pain lacing through his back, and walked over to it.

"North County branch, James speaking."

"James, hi, it's Zach."

Zach... Zach... "Oh, hi," James said, the voice falling into place.

"I heard about the accident and wanted to check in and make sure you were okay," Zach Delinsky said.

"I'm fine, thanks. Wait, how'd you get this number?"

Zach laughed, waving aside James's question with just his light voice. "It's not a business call," he said. "I'm just checking out of concern. I know your accident happened the same way my family's have."

"Right, yeah," James said. "Well, I'm fine."

"Good. I was worried about you."

This wasn't flirting, either. This was just a call of concern. No big deal, Gabriella didn't need to know about it.

"Do you need anything?" Zach continued. "Anything at all, just let me know."

"No, I really don't," James said. "But thank you."

"Medical bills? You can send them our way. I'll make sure they go through the system."

"The Foundation's covering it," James said. "Really, I'm fine."

"Just making sure you're taken care of," Zach said. "Between that and dealing with my family over the past few days..."

James laughed a little, the tightness in his chest easing somewhat. "I met... oh, I've lost track. But there were a few older ones and a younger one and they were not happy to meet me."

"The younger one's my cousin, James," Zach said, voice easy like they were just catching up. "He's a good kid. Nervous, though."

James thought back to the way the kid had cowered beside the Foundation agent. "I don't blame him, though."

"Oh, no. No. But he's always been like that."

They spent a few more minutes on the phone together and finally, James had to hang up. He put the phone back down and prayed it would stay silent long enough for him to catch his breath.

He missed his phone, now dust at the bottom of some overhang on the South Shore. Maybe the Foundation would cover the cost of a new one, since he lost his while doing their work. He got up and walked into his office, letting the door stay open behind him.

The couch Aunt Bev had pawned off on him was sitting just inside the entrance, pressed up against a bare wall. It was ugly, but extremely comfortable. When she'd offered it up, he hadn't wanted it at first. But then he needed some more seating in his office, and the couch was kind of cozy. Made the room a little less simultaneously spooky and sterile. So he'd enlisted Graham and Amelia to help him get it, and now it was, as Amelia put it, the showpiece of his office.

The computer slowly turned on as James sat down in his desk chair. He hadn't lied, he wasn't going to do much today, especially if Amelia was getting out of the hospital. But he'd catch up on his email. Then maybe he'd grab a nap on that couch so he could stay in the loop without getting yelled at for working.

Chapter 14

Amelia came by Headquarters with Madelyn around four that afternoon. James was sitting at his desk, trying not to scream at the rejected reimbursement form, as he heard the front door open. He hurried out to see Amelia walking up the stairs as Madelyn closed the door behind them. She had a few butterfly bandages across her forehead and a cast on her arm and looked exhausted as she smiled up at James.

"Hey," she said, walking up the steps and crossing the living room.

She hugged him gently, and he wrapped his arms around her with equal care. She was alive. He hadn't disbelieved it, but only now that she was in the room did he realize how much tension he'd been holding.

They spent a few minutes on the couch, comparing notes. Amelia had spent a mostly sleepless night at the hospital, so she and Madelyn were going home from here and she'd be off tomorrow. James had a feeling he was going to be off as well, whether or not he wanted to be.

Their stories lined up, to James's relief. He trusted himself as much as he could to remember how things had really gone. But he was grateful both for the backup and the confirmation that neither of them had any lost time. While he'd dismissed Gabriella's concerns about mind control, the thought had lingered as he'd tried to nap on the couch in his office earlier.

James left a few minutes after Amelia, heading out the door just as Graham was coming down the stairs too. "Ready?" Graham asked.

Oh right, Chris's roommate interview. James sighed. "Yeah," he said. "As I'm going to be."

He took his time heading home, but it wasn't enough time. It would never be enough time. He just wanted to go to bed, but when he got there, Chris caught him at the door.

"Hey bro," he said. "Heard about the accident. You okay?"

"Yeah, just a little banged up," James replied.

"Cool cool. Uh, Roger's gonna be here in a few minutes, so are you good to meet him?"

No. No, he wasn't. But the words that came out were, "Yeah, that's fine."

"Cool."

James went to his room to change, gazing longingly at his bed as he pulled on clean clothes. When he came out, Graham was walking in. He gave James a look. "Let's just give it a chance."

Graham was kinder than he was. Or just eager to not split their rent by two for the foreseeable future.

The buzzer sounded a few minutes later, just after James managed to shovel some leftover pasta into his mouth. A moment later, Chris was leading Roger into the apartment.

"Not bad, not bad," Roger said, looking around and nodding. "I could do a lot with this."

Graham turned and looked blankly at James. Roger came into the room, then jumped like he was startled to see them there.

"James, Graham, this is Roger. He's looking for a place."

James shook Roger's hand. It was sweaty, and he resisted the urge to wipe his own hand on his pants after letting go.

"So Roger," Graham said, shaking his hand as well. "Tell me about yourself."

"What do you need to know?"

"Uh, what do you do for work?" Graham asked. "What kinds of things are you looking for in roommates?"

"Why do you fucking care what I do for work?" Roger snapped suddenly. "You know, work isn't all there is to life."

Graham stepped back, holding up his hands. "Shit, sorry," he said. "I just mean, tell me about yourself."

"I'm a whole person, that's who I am," Roger said, still heated. "My 'job' or 'career' is only a small portion of that person. And it pisses me off when people don't appreciate that."

"Look, man, we're just trying to get to know you," James said, subtly shifting his body in between Roger and Graham.

Roger smiled at them, showing full teeth. "Oh, totally. Okay," he said. "I'm a person, a spirit in a corporeal form, enjoying the world as it is and on my own terms."

"And what will you be doing to, um, pay rent?" James asked.

"Is that all you two care about, fucking money?" Roger demanded.

Something throbbed behind James's eye. "Alright," he said. "I'm done. Roger, nice to meet you, but this isn't going to work out. Have a good night."

Roger shook his head. "Slaves to the almighty dollar. It's pathetic."

Chris went to walk him out, but he was already storming toward the door. He slammed it shut behind himself, then James heard his footsteps smashing down the stairs of their triple-decker.

James and Graham looked at each other, then both looked at Chris. "Where did you find him?" James asked, forcing his voice to stay even.

"He's a buddy's brother," Chris said casually. "Sorry it didn't work out. I thought he'd be good."

"Had you met him before?" Graham asked, voice incredulous.

"Nah."

James shook his head. There were plenty of things he could say right now, but none of them felt worth it. So instead, he walked into his room, closed the door, and locked it.

* * *

Both James and Amelia took the next day off. James spent it alternating between watching Netflix on the couch and taking walks in his neighborhood. It was a nice enough place, nothing special. He'd lived here for a few years and hadn't spent much time exploring outside of work. But as he walked around, hands shoved deep in his coat pockets, he thought it was fine for what it was. A little too far from downtown to walk to the shops there, but close enough to the main road that he could grab some takeout and walk home after.

Maybe a vacation would be nice, James thought as he went to bed that night. It wasn't like he had to travel. He could do this for a week, preferably with less pain coursing through his body during the actual vacation.

The next day, he felt a little better. Still sore, but walking the day before had helped a lot. He felt more limber as he went into Headquarters and then felt better still when he saw Amelia there, sitting on the couch with a cup of coffee.

"So what do you think?" she asked as he sat down next to her with the iced coffee he'd bought on his way in.

"What do you mean?"

"What caused the accident?"

James shrugged. "I mean, it could be a few different things."

"But we both know that it's connected with the Delinsky case."

"Yeah."

"It's a curse," Amelia said. "We all think so. And someone doesn't want us solving this."

"I think it's that same guy that wanted us out of the Foxborough store," James said. "He and I got into a disagreement and we nearly died immediately after? It was sloppy. Not the work of a professional. I'm going back today to talk to him."

"That's a terrible idea."

"No, I'll play it safe. Amulets, holy water, setting up personal wards beforehand. I'll do everything I can to block out curses. We should have done that before and I'm sorry I didn't think of it."

Amelia shook her head. "Not your fault," she said. "We both could have thought of it and didn't."

"Yeah, but I'm the captain. So it ends with me."

They were quiet for a second. "Speaking of," James said. "Have you thought any more about the Hillsborough position?"

Amelia shrugged. "I guess."

"And?"

"And I just got out of the hospital after an overnight stay to watch for brain damage, and you and I nearly died. I haven't put that much thought in. I'll do more once the case is done."

Guilt slipped into James's stomach. "Fair," he said. "Sorry, I won't bring it up again."

"No, it's fine," Amelia said. "Really."

James felt like he should say something else, but just took a sip of his coffee. "What are you feeling up to doing today?" he asked.

Amelia thought for a second. "Honestly," James added.

She glared at him, then sighed. "Honestly," she said. "I think I'm better off staying at Headquarters today. I think the Foundation sent over the details we were looking for. So I can look through those. Gabriella and Graham can take anything new that comes in."

"I'll go to Foxborough and beat the information out of that Jeremy asshole if I have to," James said. "I'll see if Bradley wants to come, so I have backup."

"Guy's gonna shit his pants when he sees you two roll up in your Chevy."

"Fuck off," James said, nudging her with his knee.

"I'm glad you're not dead," Amelia said.

"Right back at you."

* * *

"Bradley."

James walked over to the back bedroom, where he could see Bradley sitting at the desk, frowning over a notebook. He was whispering something under his breath as he read and didn't look up as James walked closer.

"Brad?"

Bradley jumped, spinning toward the door and glaring at James. "What the fuck, McManus?"

James held up his hands. "Hey, I've been trying to get your attention for like thirty seconds. Are you okay?"

"Yeah, I'm fine. What do you need?"

"I'm heading to Foxborough. Do you still want to go?"

"Yeah, fine. Hang on."

Bradley closed the notebook in front of him, then closed a window on his computer before standing up. "Let me get my coat."

"You'll need it. It's freezing and we're about to go battle the Christmas shopping crowd."

Bradley grimaced. "I'm going to need coffee for that," he said.

James had just finished the one he brought with him, but he was feeling that need now, too. "Yeah," he said. "We'll stop at Dunks, then go crack some skulls."

* * *

"Are we getting in?"

A few minutes later, James and Bradley were standing outside of James's car. James had the keys in his hand and the door was unlocked. He just needed to get in and start the car. It was nothing. He'd driven here this morning without much fear. Nothing had changed now that they were going back to Foxborough.

"Yeah," he said, his breath a cloud in the bitter air. "Yeah."

Bradley's voice was impatient, and he scowled at James. "Look," he said. "Is this a thing? Do you want me to drive? My car is right there."

He jabbed a gloved finger over at his car parked along the sidewalk. James didn't want to take his offer, he just needed to get into his own car. "No, I'm fine," he said. "If I don't do it, I never will."

"Inspirational."

James ignored him and slid into the driver's seat. The familiarity of his car was comforting. It was lower to the ground, and he'd been driving it for years.

It was fine. They'd take a different route, and it'd be fine.

"We should get driving first, then stop for coffee," Bradley said as James backed out of the driveway. "Don't hit my car."

"I'm not going to hit your fucking car," James snapped as he backed around it and into the road.

"Good, because the Foundation won't compensate me for it."

"Yeah, they're not paying for my new phone. So they're sure as shit not going to pay if I back into your Corolla."

Bradley looked at him. "They're not replacing your phone?"

"Of course not," James said with a sigh. "I only lost it when a curse caused my brakes to fail and the company van to go over an embankment."

Bradley was silent for a second and James waited for whatever complaint about either him or the Foundation that was about to come. But nothing did. He glanced over and saw Bradley looking out the window as they left their neighborhood.

"You good?" he asked as they turned and started passing Fairview Hills Cemetery on their right.

"Huh? Yeah, fine. I'll talk to them about your phone."

Bradley looked tired, but so didn't they all. So James dropped it and headed toward the highway.

Chapter 15

An hour later, James was pulling into a spot at the far end of the crowded mall parking lot. Just like the other day, it had been murder trying to get in. Cars lined up and crept slowly through the lot, drivers fighting each other over parking spots as they blocked in the person who was currently trying to get out of the spot they fought over. James didn't think Bradley would go into the shop and start killing people while he found a parking space, but he didn't know that for sure. So instead, he parked first.

"Listen, keep things calm," James said. "I don't know what kind of power this guy has or how he has it. But he killed two people and tried to kill three others at least. So don't fuck around with him."

"I'm a professional," Bradley said, sliding an amulet over his neck.

"I know," James said as he hooked a blessed pin onto his coat. "But still."

"Fine."

A moment later, James was confident that they had every protection they possibly could have on their bodies. He walked into Delinsky's and immediately, his confidence wavered. It was exactly the same as it had been. Christmas carols sang cheerfully in the lightly scented air and he felt extremely angry and very poor standing here in the doorway.

He glanced over at Bradley, who was looking around the store with feigned polite interest. He looked like he fit right in, like he wouldn't go pale at the price tags here. James had seen his apartment and knew Bradley wasn't any wealthier than he was. But he looked like he belonged in this world.

This world sucks, James reminded himself. It's full of rich people making themselves richer at the expense of their employees. And maybe some of those employees had had enough and turned to murder.

James looked toward the row of registers and saw no Jeremy, but the woman from the other day was there. She was ringing someone out, her hair hanging in her face. As she looked up for the next customer, she saw James. Even from here, he could see her eyes widen. She looked to her left and James followed her gaze to see Jeremy standing by a rack of Christmas dresses.

Something hot flashed in James's face as he looked at Jeremy. Before he quite realized what he was doing, he was walking over to him. After the car ride, he was aching again, and feeling it just made him angrier.

Jeremy looked over and James saw a flash of panic mingled with anger as James approached him. He went to say something, but then James had him by his collar, grabbing handfuls of his shirt and steering him toward the gleaming gold wall behind him.

"Surprised to see me, asshole?" James snapped as he shoved Jeremy against the wall.

"What the—" Jeremy started to say, but James cut him off.

"It didn't work," he said. "Whatever you did, it didn't work. But you nearly killed my best friend. What the fuck did you do?"

"Nothing," Jeremy said.

His tone was sneering, but James could see the fear in his eyes. "Get your hands off me," Jeremy snapped.

Right. James had just attacked an employee. He knew why, and Jeremy clearly knew why, but anyone who saw them wouldn't. They'd assume James wanted a refund or something. Thankfully, nobody seemed to be looking except the woman at the register, who seemed terrified. James let go of Jeremy.

"You tried to kill us," he said.

"You can't prove that," Jeremy snapped.

"Sure we can," Bradley said from where he'd apparently materialized beside James. "Come on."

He nudged James painfully in the side and started to walk away. James turned with him, then looked over his shoulder at Jeremy.

"You're lucky," he said. "But you can't stay lucky forever."

Jeremy laughed bitterly. "Yeah, lucky," he said. "Fuck off."

He stormed away and Bradley stopped and jabbed James again. "Let's go," he snapped.

He walked out of the store with an air of dignity that James had never actually seen work in context before. James followed after him, trying to ignore the stares from customers.

"Wow," Bradley said as soon as they were out the door.

"Don't start," James warned him.

"Bradley, don't do anything stupid. Bradley, be professional," Bradley continued, adjusting his scarf as they walked. "Bradley, don't assault the cashier."

"He nearly killed Amelia," James retorted, face burning in the cold air.

"Besides, maybe he's not the one we need to talk to," Bradley said.

"What do you mean?"

"While you were busy manhandling that guy, did you happen to notice the woman who clearly knew exactly what was going on?" Bradley asked him as they walked back to the car.

An SUV passed at an alarming speed and Bradley flipped off the driver as he turned to James with an eyebrow raised.

"That young woman," James said. "She was there the other day, too. Do you think maybe they're working together?"

"That's exactly what I'm thinking," Bradley said. "And if he's not going to talk to us, neither is she. But they're scared."

"Let's bring this to the Foundation," James said. "Maybe they'll have some connection here that we can't access."

They got into the car a moment later and James tried not to think about the way the sky looked the same today as it had the other day when he and Amelia had been here. Heavy clouds that promised snow and ice on the road ahead, whether the forecast had called for it or not. They weren't going to drive the same route back. Instead, they'd just get on the highway and keep all of their protections on until they got into the safety of Headquarters.

"We should ask the Delinskys for access to their employees," James said, turning out of the lot. "Not that it'll get us far, but "

Someone ran out in front of the car and he stopped short, inches from hitting them.

"WHAT THE FUCK?" he screamed as he put the car in park and got out.

It was the young woman from Delinsky's. She was out of breath and hadn't stopped to put on a coat. The name tag on her striped shirt read JANIS.

"Leave us alone," she demanded.

"Are you insane?" James snapped. "I almost hit you."

"I mean it," Janis said, voice trembling. "Just stop. Or next time you might not survive."

"So it was you," Bradley said, voice low on the other side of the car. "How'd you do it?"

"I didn't do anything!"

"Right."

"Listen, they aren't good people," Janis said. She was young, she couldn't have been any older than twenty-three, if that. "They hurt people, good people. And you should be careful if you don't want to get hurt with them."

"What do you know?" James asked. "Come on, you know this is wrong. Tell us everything and we can help keep you safe."

The woman shook her head. "No," she said. "I didn't do anything. Neither did Jeremy."

"So, someone did it for you?" Bradley asked.

The woman was silent. "Right," James said. "Who was it? Did you hire someone?"

"I don't have to tell you anything."

James sighed. "Listen," he said. "Of course they suck. We all know that. But you don't get to play judge, jury, and executioner."

"What, and they can?"

"What do you mean?"

"They mess with people's lives and don't give a shit about the consequences," the woman said. "So you know what? Maybe they should be scared for once."

Before James could say anything else, she darted away, back toward the safety of the mall. Bradley went to chase her, but James shook his head. "Forget it," he said. "She's not going to say anything else."

"Did she really think that would work?" Bradley asked.

James shrugged. "I mean, maybe?" he said. "Neither of them seem like criminal masterminds. But if they hired someone, that could bring an extra layer of trouble into this mess."

They got back into the car and James started driving again. "Do you think the Foundation would have information on, like, curse casters for hire?" he asked Bradley.

"Maybe," Bradley said. "But I don't know if they'd have any official contact information. That seems like something they'd tried to suppress rather than collaborate with."

"My Uncle Tommy said he might have some contacts who could help with curses," James said, slowing down and pausing before a stop sign.

Bradley turned to him. "Excuse me?"

"I said my Uncle Tommy might be able to help us."

"Your Uncle Tommy," Bradley repeated slowly.

"What?" James replied defensively. "Just if the Foundation doesn't have options, maybe we can talk to him."

"I'm sure the Foundation would love that."

"Well, maybe they should give us the resources we need. It's not like there's not a solution here."

"Want to toss a curse and murder our higher-ups?" Bradley asked.

James turned to him. "Jesus Christ," he said. "Where did that come from?"

"That's what those two are doing with the Delinskys," Bradley said. "Underpaid, overworked, under-supported. Sound familiar?"

"Are you saying that maybe they have a point?" James asked.

"Not that they should murder people," Bradley said. "But the anger was familiar, wasn't it?"

"This isn't Robin," James said. "But it's damn similar, huh?"

"They're not trying to get better support though," Bradley said. "They just want revenge."

The joke was almost out of James's mouth, but now wasn't the time. Sure, some days he wanted revenge. But he'd never considered murder. That was too fucking far. "What do you think?" he asked. "Should we talk to Uncle Tommy?"

Bradley looked at him for a long moment. "Let's start with our actual workplace first," he said, voice dripping with condescension, "Then we'll decide on Uncle Tommy measures from there."

James nodded and resisted the urge to push Bradley out of the car.

Chapter 16

James had a meeting with McGovern that afternoon and got back about ten minutes before it was supposed to start. So, rather than try to get anything done before it began, he headed into his office. Maybe he could catch up on email or something while he waited.

He walked into the office, glanced over at the couch, and stepped back, startled. Amelia was lying there with her eyes closed. Her casted arm rested on her chest while her other arm was thrown over her head, against the threadbare green throw pillow he'd put there a few days ago. She was breathing evenly, and James moved carefully to avoid waking her up.

The demon books were still missing from the bookshelf as he walked past, and the dirt that had scattered from the shelf crunched under his thick wool socks. James winced at the sensation. Normally, he was completely on board with no outside shoes indoors. But he was either going to have to actually vacuum his floor or change that rule.

If Gabriella was going to be their researcher, he'd need to get her input on more books to purchase for their excuse for a library. Maybe they could squeeze a little bit out of the budget to update some of these more... antique resources. Once they were done dealing with the Delinskys, he'd turn his focus toward that.

As he got to his desk, he heard Amelia shifting on the couch. He turned to see her crack an eye open and look at him.

"You okay?" James asked, stopping before he sat down in his chair.

She nodded, closing her eyes again. "Fine," she said.

"I've got a meeting in a few minutes, but you can stay there if you want."

She took a deep breath, then opened her eyes. "Nah," she said. "I'm up. I'm just on my break."

Amelia sat up, folding her knees as she leaned against the puffy back cushion of the sofa. "Bradley called," she said.

"When?"

"When you were getting gas. He said you attacked the guy at the store?"

"The one that tried to kill us? Yeah."

"That was stupid."

James sighed, then walked over and sat down next to her on the couch. "I know."

"For real, are you okay?"

He wanted to say he was fine and move on. But instead, he shrugged. "Honestly, no clue," he said. "We both were almost murdered when a curse destroyed our brakes and I'm not sure if I'm traumatized by it or not. And now we've got people murdering their bosses and their bosses suck. Like, they're fucking awful and should face some kind of consequence. But nobody gets to decide that someone else deserves to die, you know? Right now I hate our client, hate our suspects, and hate that the Foundation is putting so much on us. So just a regular day."

Amelia nodded and he could tell just from her face that she was feeling everything he'd just said. "Now what?" she asked.

"I have a meeting with McGovern in a few minutes," James said. "I'm going to see what the Foundation can do about tracking down someone who sets curses for money."

"Want me to stay?"

"Do you have anything else going on?"

Amelia shook her head. "Not really," she said. "Graham and Gabriella went to go take a statement about a haunted house over by the high school. I need to do my workout at some point today, but I'm not in a hurry."

"Me too," James said. "I've fallen off of it so bad. I assume you're just going to walk?"

"Nah, I'm thinking of free weights. Maybe some pull-ups."

James rolled his eyes and huffed a laugh. Then he got up and headed toward the computer for the meeting.

* * *

"James!" McGovern said a few minutes later over the video chat. "And Amelia! You two look good. How are you feeling?"

"Alive," Amelia said with a small laugh.

"Same," James said.

"That's good, I suppose," McGovern said. "Alright, just a couple of things to go over. James, I'm sorry, but the Foundation doesn't cover personal tech that was damaged in the field."

"Even if I need it for work?"

"We can loan you a Foundation phone," McGovern offered.

He'd seen them and he was better off with the cordless phone they still had for the landline. "Thank you anyway."

"Next, your reports are all set. I have a copy of the police report as well. The van has been declared totaled, so we'll work on that. I was sure that our partner garages would have someone who could fix it, but apparently, it was too damaged."

It was also probably halfway to totaled before it went off that embankment. Still, a sharp pang went through James at the official loss of the van. It was ridiculous, he knew. But it was a little like losing a team member.

"James, there was a small note of concern. The police had you take a breathalyzer test?"

The memory of the cop's harshness and the swirling confusion of the accident threatened to make him vomit right here at his desk. But instead, James nodded. "Yeah."

"You weren't drinking on a case, of course."

"Of course not!"

"That's what the report said," McGovern said.

Then why say anything about it at all? James's heart was pounding, and he took a deep breath, trying to push away the humiliation. "I was in shock and disoriented because the brakes failed on the van and sent us off the road. I wasn't intoxicated."

"Nor do we think so."

Then why was this a topic of discussion? "Is there anything else?" Amelia asked quickly, rescuing him before either he or McGovern could say anything else on the topic.

"Only new business if you have it. Do you have something to bring up?"

"Yes," James said, sitting up a little straighter. "I sent over the update, but we have solid reason to believe it's a curse that's targeting the Delinsky family. We think that someone hired a professional."

"A professional conjurer?"

"I guess you could put it that way," James said. "But what kinds of resources does the Foundation have to track down someone who would do that?"

McGovern took off his glasses and polished them on his shirt. Then he put them back on his face with a sigh. "We certainly know of people we've stopped from doing that kind of work," he said. "But if you're hoping for a directory of sorts, no, we don't have that."

"What would you suggest we do, then?" James asked, trying to keep his frustration out of his voice.

"Maybe some of the other branches know," McGovern said, clearly struggling for suggestions. "Or local covens."

Yeah, there was an idea. Go to a group of harmless witches who had no reason to hate them, then stir up shit by asking if they knew of any evil witches that might kill people for money. Amelia looked equally grim at the idea, but she nodded. "We'll consider those," she said. "Thanks."

"Anything else?"

There wasn't, so they ended the meeting a moment later. As soon as the screen went dark, James buried his face in his hands. "Jesus, that was useless."

He lifted his head. "Want to insult some potential allies?"

"Absolutely not," Amelia said.

"My Uncle Tommy offered to help if we needed it."

"The vampire hunter?"

"In a manner of speaking."

"Yeah, I'm game," Amelia said. "Give him a call and see what he knows."

* * *

The phone rang about eight times as James considered just hanging up. Did Uncle Tommy not have a voicemail? James was about seventy percent sure this was a landline, too. Had he just not set it up?

"Hello?"

Uncle Tommy's gruff, booming voice suddenly replaced the quiet ringing. "Hi, Uncle Tommy, it's James."

"Hey, kiddo, what's up?"

"So you said you know some people who could help with the curse aspect of this?"

Uncle Tommy laughed and James moved his head away from the phone, just a little. "Foundation didn't have what you needed, huh?"

"No," James said, glancing around the room to see if any of the others were there. "They, um, apparently don't keep directories of people who would curse for money."

"Now let me see..." Uncle Tommy's voice was exaggeratedly thoughtful as James heard him shuffling around. "MARY! Have you seen my directory of people who cast curses for money?"

James didn't catch what his aunt said in reply, but apparently, it was rude enough to elicit another booming laugh. "Hang on, Jimmy," Uncle Tommy said.

He set the phone down, and James heard the sounds of rummaging and mumbling. After a moment, he was back.

"I've got some names for you," Uncle Tommy said. "Let me take a look... dead, gone, um, looks like I got a name for you."

"Oh?"

"Polly Grace, out in Ashburnham."

"Ashburnham?"

"Yeah. Nice place. Have you ever been?"

James rolled his eyes. "No, the case I'm working on is in Ashburnham."

"The case... wait, kid, don't tell me you're looking at the Delinsky thing."

James didn't technically tell him, so he couldn't get in trouble, right? They didn't record on this phone. He knew that for a fact because it had broken and the Foundation had been promising to fix their recording tech for years now. "I guess you could say that," he said.

Another laugh so loud that James flinched. "Yeah, I should've guessed. Okay, as far as I can tell, if you want the curse removed, you're gonna have to get her to do it. She probably tied it to the family through their place up there. But I'll warn ya, she's an odd duck. And not very friendly, which you might've already guessed."

It was like being ten years old again. "Yeah, I guessed it."

"So you should be careful if you try to contact her. If it was her that put the whammy on your brakes, you know what she's capable of. At least when she's being paid for it."

James wondered briefly how much they'd paid to have him and Amelia killed. Apparently not enough to get the good stuff. Maybe he should be offended by that. "Thanks, Uncle Tommy," he said. "I'll bring this to the team and we'll figure it out."

"That Delinsky compound is a hell of a place, huh?" Uncle Tommy said. "Have you been in it?"

"Yeah, it's disgusting," James laughed. "They called it The Cottage."

"Who needs that much space?" Uncle Tommy said. "Alright, kid, have a good night. Call me if you need anything. And don't tell your mom I told you all this."

"I'm in my thirties now. I'm allowed to work cases," James reminded him. "In fact, I'm in charge of them."

Another braying laugh. "I know, kid, I know. All right, take care."

They got off the phone, and James shook his head. There was something about talking to his aunts and uncles, no matter how old he got, that always made him feel like a child.

Chapter 17

"Hey, I need to talk to you."

"Oh God, what about?"

Graham was sitting on the couch eating a sandwich when James walked out of his office. He looked up at James cautiously. "Do you need me to come in there, or…"

He gestured toward the sandwich wrapper laid out on the coffee table, with his bag of chips and soft drink on top of it. "Oh, no," James said. "No, I can come out here."

He took one of the chairs by the computers and turned it to face Graham. It was quiet in Headquarters right now, with everybody else working on other things. Graham watched him apprehensively as he sat down.

"Stop looking at me like I'm about to murder you," James said. "This has nothing to do with Chris."

"Oh, thank God," Graham said. "I thought you were about to tell me you were moving, too."

James laughed. "I can't afford my own place," he said. "No, this is work-related. Amelia and I were talking the other day. We're thinking about getting the team more specialized, trying to split the work up a little more efficiently."

Graham nodded, reaching into his tiny chip bag for a Dorito. "That sounds cool," he said.

"Yeah, Brad's been doing logistics and finance for years, but a lot of teams have everybody choose a specialty, and it seems to work well for them. I'm thinking Gabriella on research since she's basically our researcher in everything but the title right now. And I want to talk to Madelyn later today about tech."

"Good call," Graham said. "She's been studying for that tech seminar pretty much nonstop lately."

"Do you have anything you'd be particularly interested in?" James asked.

"I refuse to be team psychologist," Graham said. "I left that life behind, and I don't want to know any of your weird secrets."

"Done," James said. "I know you're still pretty early in, so don't feel like you have to choose something now. But if there's anything that's really caught your eye since you've been here–"

"Cryptids," Graham interrupted.

He ate another chip, nodding. "Yeah, I think I'd like to learn more about cryptids. Something about almost getting eaten by a bear monster on campus last summer really sparked a new love in me."

James could have kicked himself for not thinking of it sooner. Of course they needed someone to focus on cryptids. Leominster State Forest was, like, a mile from them, and it was teeming with weird creatures. "That... sounds perfect," he said. "I'll look into what the Foundation offers for training on cryptids. I know there are a lot of workshops and modules and stuff. So we can put something together for you if they haven't done it already."

"Even if they have a program set up, I'm not sure I trust it," Graham said. "Did you know that the new agent training program thinks we're in New Bedford? I learned more about sea monsters than I did about anything that might show up on Fitchburg State's campus."

James wished he could be surprised by that. But instead, he just laughed and took one of Graham's chips.

* * *

Gabriella was next. While James was all but positive she'd say yes to becoming the team's official researcher, he didn't want to make any assumptions before sending his proposal over to McGovern. So, before he left for the night, he made his way over to the pink bedroom and knocked on the open door.

Gabriella looked up from a demonology book he recognized from his office bookshelf. "Hey," she said, setting down her pen. "What's up?"

"I'm heading out in a few minutes and just wanted to talk to you real quick."

She looked nervous at that, and he waved it aside. "It's not bad," he said. "You're not in trouble or anything. What are you working on?"

Relieved, she glanced back down at her book, where a sketch of a demon munching a human arm looked back up at them. "Just working through all the resources we have on demons," she said. "I know that the Carr case is over, but I wanted to get a full collection of notes together before working with Bradley to set up more educational material."

She glanced out the door, then lowered her voice. "I don't want to hear about it if I'm missing something."

James laughed, then glanced down the empty hallway too. He stepped inside and closed the door. "Yeah, he's in a mood lately," he said. "But hey, that actually ties in with what I wanted to discuss."

"Yeah?"

"Yeah. So, listen. Amelia and I were thinking we want to get the team more specialized. You're already basically our team researcher. But what would you think of making it official?"

Gabriella's face lit up for a moment, then she schooled her features into something more professional. "I'd love that," she said. "Um, what would you need from me?"

"Input on creating the position," James said. "I guess that's pretty much it. Like I said, you're already doing the work."

She nodded, but he could see her trying not to smile too broadly. "We'll get everything official once this Delinsky nightmare is over," he said. "But take some time to think about it, okay?"

"Absolutely."

"Do you need anything before I head out?"

Gabriella shook her head. "Nope, it's me and Madelyn tonight. So I'm going to just keep working on this unless anything comes in. You're going home, right?"

Any crack he was about to make died on his lips at the stern look on her face. "Yeah," he said instead. "Yeah, I'm heading home now."

She immediately brightened. "Oh good. Have a good night!"

She turned back to her work as James opened the door and walked out of the room, feeling slightly unsettled. When, exactly, had his baby cousin Gabriella gotten scary?

* * *

The next morning, James had a meeting scheduled with Madelyn to discuss setting her up with an official specialization as well. So of course, his work shirt had vanished. He'd gotten out of the shower, come into the bedroom to get dressed, and the button-down shirt he'd laid out for the day had disappeared from the top of the dresser.

Goddammit, he didn't have a backup and his workout shirt stank of sweat. And now here he was, standing shirtless in the middle of the room, glaring at the empty space where his shirt had been. He'd told Madelyn he wanted to meet with her at nine, then given himself plenty of time before that to clean up after his workout. Now he was running late and wasting her time.

He looked on either side of the dresser. No luck. He really needed to bring a backup in again. Maybe Graham had one. Or Bradley. Not that any of them were the same size, but he could deal with it for a day.

This place couldn't be haunted, there were too many protections up. Anything powerful enough to get past them would have much more malicious things in mind than stealing his shirt. No, it had to be here somewhere, and he was going to find it.

Ah! He pulled back the dresser from the wall and breathed a sigh of relief as he saw the shirt crunched on the floor at the bottom. He fished it out, then pulled it on. It was a little dusty and wrinkled, but whatever. He'd deal with it later.

James walked out of the bedroom, fastening the top buttons as he walked.

Madelyn was nowhere to be seen, but it was no big deal. If she was wrapping things up from the overnight shift, he would just go wait in his office for a bit, then find her.

As he walked in, he glanced down at the couch and jumped slightly again as he saw that Madelyn was already there. She was sitting on the far end of the couch, feet on the ground and head tilted back against the cushion. Her eyes were closed, but she opened them as he walked in. "Hey."

"Hey."

He sat down on the other side of the couch. "You like my new couch? I think we've all fallen asleep on it by this point."

"Yeah, it's comfortable. I figured I'd wait for you here since I wasn't sure when you'd be done."

Her voice was low, a clear sign she was having a rough day. Even after six months, James still didn't know exactly how she wanted to handle these things. But considering what they were going to be talking about, he'd need to.

"So what did you want to talk to me about?" she asked.

"You mentioned a while back that you were doing the Foundation's technology program," James said. "I was wondering what you would think of specializing further and becoming our team tech person."

She raised her eyebrows at him, tucking a stray lock of short, dark hair behind her ear. "What would that mean?"

"I don't know all the details yet," he admitted. "But I want us to get a bit more specialized than we are now. I don't think anyone can make our computers run well, not unless we have a magic division in-house. But the Foundation keeps talking about different tech they're sending our way while we're still trying to figure out how to incorporate what they've already sent. You've got a head for that stuff and I can barely get my phone to work."

Madelyn laughed, then paused. "Would I be out of the field for good?" she asked.

"I don't want you to be," James said. "Unless you think it would be best."

"I don't," she said quickly. "No, I want to be back out there. I don't know when, but doing observations and interviews has made me feel more like I'm part of things again."

James wanted to jump on that immediately, to tell her she'd always been part of things. But he knew that despite the rest of the team's best efforts, things had changed.

"You don't have to answer this," James said. "But have the doctors given you any kind of prognosis?"

He cringed a little, but she didn't seem to mind the question. "I mean, I'm going to live, if that's what you mean."

He shot her a look. "Not even a little."

"Sorry." But she didn't look sorry. "No, I mean, we don't know? It'll probably never fully go away, but I'm hoping it'll get easier to function with time. I'm in treatment and it's going well. And by now I've come to grips with the fact that this is my life. But I need to keep going at it as though I'm definitely going to get back out in the field regularly at some point. Does that make sense?"

"Completely," he said. "So, how about this? You think about the technology thing-"

"I don't need to," Madelyn interrupted. "I'm in."

"Awesome. We'll figure that process out between the two of us. Maybe Bradley too. And we keep on with your plan. As long as you're safe and healthy, I'm open to any ideas you have about fieldwork."

Madelyn smiled at him. "What?" he asked.

"You're a good captain," she said. "Not that I thought you wouldn't be. But... you're good at this."

"I just lost my shirt behind the dresser for five minutes. Don't be so confident."

She laughed and stood up. "I'm going to get ready to go," she said. "Do you need anything before the end of my shift?"

James shook his head. "Nope," he said. "I'll see you tomorrow."

"Bye."

She left, and he stretched out on the couch for a moment, putting his hands behind his head. There was a lot to do today, but he could take a moment before the Delinskys and their bullshit needed to be dealt with.

Chapter 18

Later that day, James had an address in hand for Polly Grace, along with a printout of directions and very scant information on her. There were rumors online, just a few mentions in different Facebook groups of work for hire that she'd do. They said it was embroidery, but it seemed oddly coded. Not that it mattered. James was going to go to the source and get an honest answer about whatever the hell was going on here.

"Hey, Amelia," he called.

She'd been on the couch when he went into his office, but now she was nowhere to be found. He glanced into the messy kitchen, found it empty, then headed down toward the gym.

Muffled pop punk was pouring out from the crack beneath the door and when he opened it, he found Amelia and Madelyn walking slowly on the treadmills together. He waved and motioned to the stereo. Amelia gave him a nod, and he turned it off.

"How's it going?" he asked.

"Not bad," Amelia said.

She gestured with her injured arm. "It's a little difficult to keep my balance, but I'm getting better."

"Hold on to the safety rail," James said.

"Yes, Dad."

He rolled his eyes. "I'm going to go check out this Polly Grace woman. Want to come?"

"When?"

"Half an hour or so?"

She grimaced. "You didn't get my note?"

"No, what's up?"

"Graham's taking the second half of my shift. I'm going to go up to Hillsborough to observe their team."

James didn't like how that statement made his chest go tight. Why was it an issue? She'd made no secrets that she wanted to be a captain and if she'd been hesitant the past few days, that didn't mean she'd changed her mind. If James had convinced himself she had, then that was his problem.

"Oh, great," he said, hating the false note of cheer in his voice. "No, really, that's awesome. Just observing?"

"Yeah," she said, still walking. "They invited me up to check out their operation and just get an idea of how it works. I figure it's probably not too different from here, but it's worth going."

"Definitely, yeah," he said. "Okay, no problem. I'll see if Bradley can go with me when he gets here."

"I saw him out in his car a few minutes before I came in here," Amelia said. "So he's here a little early."

"Thanks, I'll go check."

He turned the music back on, then headed out of the gym and up the stairs to the front door. When he opened it, he immediately regretted leaving his jacket in his office, but stepped outside anyway.

He spotted Bradley in his car, where it was parked along the sidewalk, and headed over. The frozen grass crunched under his shoes and he could feel an almost-invisible flurry of snow flicking against his face. He got to the passenger side door and knocked on the window.

Bradley pulled off his headphones and scowled at James, rolling the window down. "I'm not on for another fifteen minutes," he snapped.

"I know," James said. "Sorry. But do you want to go check out this Polly Grace with me?"

"The one who curses people for money?"

"One and the same."

"Yeah, hang on."

He rolled the window back up, shoved his headphones in his bag, and slipped the bag under the seat. Then he got out and joined James on the sidewalk.

"When are we going?"

"Now?"

"Sure."

Bradley followed James over to his car, sliding into the passenger seat.

"What were you listening to?" James asked, reaching into his backseat for the spare jacket he usually stashed there.

"Nothing."

James wasn't sure why he bothered. So instead of trying to engage with Bradley when he was in this mood, he pulled out of the driveway and turned the radio up.

After a few minutes, he glanced over at Bradley, who was sitting in the passenger seat, clenching and relaxing his fists. "You sure you're okay?" James asked.

"Yes!" Bradley snapped.

"Fine, whatever, Christ."

He didn't expect an apology, so he wasn't upset when there was only silence beyond the soft music on the radio. They drove through downtown, passing the Christmas displays on the town common. The trees were wrapped in colorful lights that were turned on, even in the daylight. Beyond the trees, James could see the path was lined with lights leading to the old cemetery at the back of the common. It was sweet and comforting right now when his nerves were rubbed raw by this case.

"What's the plan when we get there?" Bradley asked.

Good question. "We ask to talk to her, I guess?"

"Oh, just walk in and ask, hey did you kill a guy? No reason, just curious? Are you fucking serious?"

James was used to a degree of attitude from Bradley, but this was above and beyond the usual, and he wasn't going to put up with it. Even if something was going on. "You don't have to go," he said, coming to a stop at a red light.

"Apparently I do if you're going to kill yourself."

"I'm not going to frigging... I'm planning to tell her I heard about her embroidery service. That's the code they're throwing around for her curses in all those awful Facebook groups."

"Oh."

"Yeah, fucking *oh*. Stop treating me like I'm stupid, I'm tired of it."

He hadn't meant to say all of that, but there was no taking it back now. He thought Bradley would come back with something nasty, but he just grimaced. "Fine," he said shortly.

Not quite an apology, but James would take it. They were clearly both on edge. "It's fine," he said. "Look, I know what I'm doing, okay?"

"Sure."

They were silent as James kept driving. The snow was more noticeable now, sticking to the roads and to his windshield. He turned on the wipers and the gentle pattern of their movements filled the car.

"So you saw the Cottage?" James said a little later as they were pulling onto the highway. "It's wild, isn't it? I've never seen a house that big."

"Yeah, it's pretty big," Bradley said.

"When they said cottage at first, I thought they were talking about a little summer place against a lake. With seventies wood paneling and shit like that. Not a palace."

Bradley's laugh was nearly silent, but it was enough that James felt some of the tension in the car ease. The music switched to some old, crackly folk song on the college station and he left it, letting the twangy guitars fill the silence for the rest of the drive.

* * *

Polly Grace's house was a tiny cottage tucked in the woods of Ashburnham. This was a real cottage, a little home that was falling apart in the ragged yard surrounding it. Dead plants poked up from the thin layer of snow that had fallen over the yard and there was rusted work equipment filling the small side space opposite the frozen garden.

James got out and tried to ignore his nerves. He was as protected as he would ever be. Father McEnerney had basically baptized him over again. He wasn't Catholic anymore, though apparently, neither was the Father these days. But between the anointing in holy oil, the amulet around his neck, and the wards he'd meditated on in the peace of the pink bedroom this morning, he was set. And he'd done everything he could to protect Bradley too, who was still grumbling slightly from his own anointing yesterday with the Father.

"Alright, you hang back and I'll talk to her," James said.

Bradley still looked skeptical, but he stepped back. Taking it for the olive branch he knew it was, James nodded, then walked up the small set of broken stairs to the front door. A faded Halloween witch hung on the door and he tried not to laugh as he knocked.

He waited for a second, listening for the sound of footsteps on the other side. Nothing. He knocked again. "Hello?" he called. "Ms. Grace? I'm here to ask about some embroidery work."

He held his breath, listening desperately for anything inside the house. If she wouldn't speak to them, how were they going to stop what was happening? Those two clowns in Foxborough weren't going to say anymore. He already had to come up with a cover story about how he found Polly Grace to avoid getting both him and Uncle Tommy in trouble. That wouldn't be a problem. It wasn't like he never fudged reports. But if he could talk to her, maybe-

Silence again. There was no car in the tiny driveway, not that it meant anything. But he tried one more time, knocking on the door as hard as he dared.

"Ma'am?" he called. "Listen, if you're in there, I'm just here about embroidery. I saw your work, and it's very fine. Can we talk?"

He glanced back at Bradley, who was watching the picture window at the front of the house with interest. Then he turned back, but the house was still silent.

"She's not home," James said, turning around and walking carefully down the broken stairs.

Bradley was still looking at the window, but he nodded and turned back to the car, face expressionless. James thought nothing of it as he slid into the driver's seat and turned on the car. They were pulling away from the house when Bradley spoke.

"The window curtain twitched," he said, voice soft as though he was afraid she might hear them still. "She was in there."

James slowed down. "Should we go back?"

"Absolutely not. If she doesn't want to talk to you now, what makes you think she will if you demand to go in?"

"Fair. Come on, let's head back and we'll regroup with the others. I need to come up with a reason why I know she exists."

"Where'd you find out?"

"Uncle Tommy."

Bradley pursed his lips, and James couldn't help smiling. "What?" he said. "I told you, he's got connections. It's fine, I'll tell them that Rosa over in Palmer had the information. I'll give her a call when we get back and ask her to cover for me. It'll be fine."

Bradley's phone rang before he could say anything. He picked up. "Hello?"

He listened for a second. "Hang on, I'm putting you on speaker. It's Amelia."

He hit the speaker button, holding the phone between himself and James. "Hey, Amelia," James said. "What's up? Aren't you in Hillsborough right now?"

"Yeah," she said, voice cautious. "I'm heading back to Headquarters now. The Foundation just called me, since your phone is still out of commission. There's been another death over at the Delinskys'."

Chapter 19

Apparently, they'd gotten to Rita Delinsky after all. As soon as James and Bradley were back in the Headquarters, Amelia told them what she'd heard. She didn't have many details, but the nurse had walked into her room and found her strangled with a noose made from a hospital johnny. It was a harsh, gross, humiliating death and nobody knew exactly how it had happened.

"They said she was fine one moment, yelling at the nurse to get her some coffee," Amelia said. "And then when she got back with it, Rita was dead."

"Jesus," James muttered, glancing down at the report the Foundation had sent over to them. There were photos included, and he flipped the page over in his lap.

The woman was awful, but that didn't mean he wanted to see her like this.

"So apparently, despite all the protection at the hospital, this woman was able to get in and kill her," Madelyn said. "What do you think?"

"I think that's pretty damn powerful. She doesn't need to be there in person to do it. And I also think she knows we're onto her," James said. "We were just at her house and she was clearly there and uninterested in chatting."

He set down the page and stood up. "Anyway," he said. "We're going over to the Cottage to talk to the family and Maria, her assistant. According to the Foundation, they're basically keeping them rounded up there to make sure that there's protection for everyone. All the Foundation's protections are active. I expect a text from Father McEnerney any minute."

As if on cue, Amelia's phone pinged with an incoming text. She glanced at it. "You're good."

"He knows mine's broken. What did he say?"

"'House is set,'" she read. "'You'll need to let us know when you get here so that Foundation security agents can escort you in.'"

"This'll be fun," Graham muttered.

"What do you think?" James said to Amelia. "Full team?"

"Yeah," she said. "We need to talk to Rita's family and touch base with the security teams about everything, so we might as well all go. The quicker we're out, the better."

* * *

They took two cars over to the Cottage. James still wasn't used to being split up like this, and he was getting a little concerned about the gas mileage his team was covering. They'd been told multiple times that the Foundation didn't cover gas in private vehicles, but it wasn't like they had a choice right now, right? So the Foundation had better pay the team back.

He tried to put the thought aside as he glanced over at Amelia in the passenger seat. "What do you think about all this?" he asked.

She looked up from her phone. "I think we're not quite in over our heads, but we're getting there," she said. "And the Foundation's not going to give us what we need."

"That's kind of where I am too," James said. "This is different from our previous cases. When was the last time we had multiple dead people and had to go outside the Foundation for vital information?"

"I mean, aside from Halloween?" Amelia said. "But that was different. This is something they expect us to do. I'm worried that eventually, these things are going to become more and more our issue. Like, next time they won't have as much security. The time after that, there will be none. Or we'll be expected to negotiate it. Or provide it ourselves. You know what I mean?"

James hadn't quite been there consciously, but from the way he readily accepted her concerns, he knew that his subconscious had clearly been gnawing on that possibility for a little while. "Do you think they'd do that?" he asked.

"I think they'd try. Especially if this goes smoothly."

"And if it doesn't?"

"Then they don't."

"I hate this."

"I know."

They were quiet for a moment. James thought about the night Gabriella had called him, sobbing, from the Leominster State Forest. That case was supposed to go poorly so that they'd be able to keep doing their jobs in the aftermath. And if they did well on this one, they risked having it taken more and more for granted that they would do it all themselves.

"We're not at that point yet though," he said after a moment of tense silence.

Madelyn had been dozing in the back seat, but he heard her shuffle and sit up a little straighter. "I don't know what you two are talking about," she said. "I'd make fantastic security."

Amelia laughed, looking back at Madelyn with affection. Madelyn smirked at her, then looked out the window. "I have to admit, I'm a little excited to see this cottage everyone keeps talking about," she said. "We used to rent a cottage up in Maine every year, but I have a feeling that this is a little different."

"Just a little," Amelia said. "Considering you and I shared a twin bed up there. I'm going to tell you now that things are slightly different in this particular cottage."

"Oh?" James said, looking at Amelia. "One bed, huh?"

"Yeah, it was really sexy," Madelyn said. "Me with my foot in Amelia's face and her snoring. Exactly like the movies."

Amelia laughed. "And your cousins sharing the bed right across the room."

"Oh, Amelia," James said as he remembered suddenly. "Sometime in your many texts today, can you please ask Rosa if she's cool with me saying I learned about Polly Grace from her?"

"I thought you learned about her from..." Amelia trailed off as she realized what was happening. "Right. Yeah, I'll text her now."

"I appreciate it," James said. "I'll have a phone soon, so I can stop asking you to take all my messages for me."

"Someday we'll have room in the budget for a secretary," Amelia said as she texted.

"Yeah, because that's so high on the priority list."

"Maybe once we're all specialized, they'll let us bring one on," Madelyn said. "Or maybe they'll just keep assuming that's all Bradley's job, too."

"I'm waiting for the day they decide one of us has to be team doctor," James said. "Then they send us a PDF and wish us luck."

"God, don't even joke about that," Amelia said with a shudder. "I've heard rumors they want to cut our medical coverage. Too many hospital visits. Which, yeah, I'm really sick of going to the emergency room. But we're fighting monsters. What do they expect?"

James tried to ignore the sick little flutter that passed through him at that idea. While most of him wanted to say that the Foundation wouldn't do that, another part of him knew it was absolutely possible. But it was just rumors right now, and he had things to focus on. So instead of continuing down that path, he tried to think of something else to talk about.

* * *

The comfortable atmosphere of the car faded almost instantly as they pulled up in front of the Cottage. Graham was driving the other car and he, Gabriella, and Bradley pulled in beside James at the back of a crowd of cars. They got out and Amelia called to let the security team know they were there. Moments later, three agents walked out the front door. They were dressed in casual clothes, but James could tell from their stance that they were Foundation trained. They steered everybody into the house, past the protections on the walls, and bolted the heavy doors behind them.

As soon as they got in, Zach Delinsky was walking toward them. He was clearly trying desperately to hold himself together. "James!" he said. "Oh my God, I'm so happy to see you all."

For a second, James thought Zach might hug him. But instead, Zach just took a shuddering breath and pasted on a professional smile.

"It's nice to see you all," he said, glancing at the team. "I'm sorry it's like this. And I'm sorry I'm a mess. I'm just…"

A small sob escaped as he exhaled. "I'm sorry," he said again. "It's just… how did it get her? I don't understand. And I don't know how we can be safe here if she wasn't safe there."

"We're figuring that out," James said, trying to keep his voice calm and professional as he reached out to give Zach a squeeze on the arm. As much as he didn't appreciate the teasing about them, he didn't dislike Zach. The man had been nothing but nice to them this whole time.

"My cousin left," Zach said, voice hoarse. "James. He just took off. He told me he was leaving, so I know he's not… not dead. But…"

Shit, he might not be safe, anyway. But James wasn't about to say that. That was probably the last thing Zach needed right now, though he was clearly well aware of it. But maybe they could contact the younger man, get him somewhere safe.

"I'm scared for the kids," Zach said, interrupting James's thoughts.

James paused, glancing at Amelia. "Kids?"

"Not mine," Zach said. "My nieces and nephews. They're so little, they don't deserve to deal with this."

"Where are they?" James asked.

"They're here," Zach said. "There's four of them, all under the age of twelve. I know my family isn't great, but they wouldn't go after innocent kids, would they?"

James wished desperately that he could say no. No, of course not. But he couldn't lie like that. So instead, he just said, "We're doing everything we can to keep them safe. The Boston branch is taking care of security, both physical and magical. And we've got a lead. We just need to figure out where to take it."

Zach's eyes widened. "What is it?" he asked.

"I can't really talk about it," James admitted.

Zach's face crumpled a little, but then he nodded. "I guess I understand," he said. "What should I do?"

"What are you doing now?"

"Staying with the kids mostly," he said. "My cousins - their parents - are in meetings with the rest of the family. They're talking about just, like, how to come back from this. It's horrible. Just stocks and profits, like it's a rough day in the economy and not something that might come after their babies."

He took another shuddering breath to pull himself together at the mention of the kids, and James felt a renewed affection. He smiled, hoping it looked reassuring and leaderly.

"It's okay," he said. "You take care of the kids. We have everything as locked up as possible. Father McEnerney is taking care of things, and there are more agents here than I've ever seen in my life. You stay with the kids and keep them calm, okay? That's what I need you to do right now."

Zach nodded and smiled at James, who felt himself genuinely smile back. Then Zach hurried away.

He glanced over at Amelia, who was watching him. "What?" he asked.

Amelia shrugged. "Nothing."

"Oh fuck off, we're working."

"I didn't say anything."

He looked at Gabriella, who just smiled. "Can we focus?" James demanded. "Come on, Yasmin is coming. I can see her on the other side of the door. Let's just do these interviews and be done here."

Chapter 20

"I can't even imagine being that wealthy," Amelia said a little while later as they drove away from the Cottage. "Like, just the idea of living in that kind of environment? Growing up in it? It doesn't seem worth the money."

"I just keep thinking of the kids," James said. "Zach was so scared for them, but their parents didn't seem to give a single fuck if their kids were safe or not. Maybe I mixed up who the parents were and who they weren't, but not a single person I spoke to mentioned concern for their children."

"Same," Amelia said.

This time, it was James, Amelia, and Bradley in James's car. Madelyn had gone to ride with Graham and Gabriella. Amelia was in the backseat while Bradley was gazing out the passenger side window.

"My family was never desperate," James said. "And we had family members that were worse off than us. But we always looked out for each other, you know? I can't imagine growing up in an environment like that. Where all the adults, save like, the staff and a single uncle, don't care about you as a person? It's gotta mess with you."

"It does."

Bradley's voice was so quiet that James almost missed it. He was still facing out the window. But then he turned and faced forward, still not looking at either of them.

"I feel guilty saying it because there are so many people who have worse problems," he said. "And we weren't on the same level as the Delinskys financially. But my family was very similar, and it was fucking awful."

James thought back to the solemn children he'd seen sitting in a playroom deep inside the house. They'd passed by it as they were leaving, and Zach had stepped out to say goodbye. James assumed the kids didn't know anything about what was happening to their family, but he'd seen the serious expression on one that couldn't have been older than six. So even if they weren't aware of the danger their family was in, the kids didn't seem to be the product of a warm environment.

"Bradley," he started. "Where are you from?"

"North Shore," Bradley replied. "Over where I used to work. I grew up in Marblehead. My father was a neurosurgeon. He was brilliant and an asshole."

"I didn't know that."

"Do you talk to your family?" Amelia asked Bradley.

"No."

He didn't elaborate and James figured that was the most they were getting out of him about it. He was shocked they'd gotten that much. After seeing the dingy apartment Bradley lived in, James had assumed that he'd grown up similar to them. But apparently not. Clearly, his childhood had been closer to that of the stone-faced children they'd seen this afternoon.

"So what's on the docket when we get back?" Amelia asked.

"Funny you mention that," James said, grateful for the change of subject. "We haven't gotten a single new case since the statement they took the other day at the haunted house. Everything paranormal in this half of the county coincidentally stopped at the same time we started this major case with lots of money involved."

"Amazing how that works," Amelia muttered, shaking her head.

"So I guess when we get back, I'm going to keep looking online, see if there's any more information about Polly Grace that might help us. Like what the fuck she thinks she's doing?"

"Father McEnerney wants to visit the house," Bradley said.

"When did he say that?"

"Before we left. I told him I'd let you know since you still don't have a goddamn phone."

"Yeah, sounds good."

There were so many things he could say right now, but Bradley still seemed out of sorts and the last thing they needed was another argument like the one from the other day that might ignite into something worse.

"I'm also going to do my workout," James said. "I feel like my joints are solidifying lately. So when we get back, I'm changing, running, and not thinking about curses for a few minutes."

The house was sealed up better than anything James had ever seen before. Those kids would be safe from the exterior monsters, at the very least. So he could be thankful for that.

* * *

Despite not running for a week, James threw himself into the workout when he got back to headquarters, putting the treadmill at a faster speed than he'd planned or done in a while. There had been some hard rock CD in the player when he turned it on and it was currently blowing out the speakers. He didn't love the music, but he was able to lose himself in that and the sound of his feet hitting the treadmill belt.

This was bullshit. These people didn't care about anything beyond profits for their stupid fucking store, even as their family members were being murdered around them. The parents weren't worried for the kids, the younger generation wasn't worried for the elders, nobody cared at all. Except for one frazzled nephew who was trying to keep the children from knowing what was happening.

And now he had to go after killers who murdered in revenge for, what, exactly? They still had their jobs. Losing their manager? Had the manager been cut during layoffs? And if so, was that really worth killing over? He wanted to ask, but there was no way to get that information short of asking Jeremy and Janis.

Unless maybe something had happened. He pressed the treadmill to a higher speed as he thought. Jeremy had said there was no manager. Could something have happened to the manager at that store?

Breathless, a little while later, James slowed down and stepped off the treadmill. He was pouring sweat, but he needed to check on this before he showered. And since he had no phone, he needed to go upstairs to do it. But if he could get the name of the manager from Zach, maybe he could get an answer.

Zach's business card was still in James's wallet, which was in his office. He stepped inside, grabbed the card, and sat down at his desk, trying to ignore the way his shirt was sticking to his chest.

The phone rang twice, then Zach picked up. "Zach Delinsky, how can I help you?"

"Zach, it's James over at the Foundation."

"James, did something happen? What's going on?"

"Actually, I had a question for you. Would you be able to get me the name of a manager from one of your stores?"

Zach paused for a second. "Of course," he said finally. "Um, hang on, let me get my laptop."

James heard the sound of children's music playing in the background and realized Zach was still on child duty. This simultaneously warmed and depressed him. "Alright," Zach said. "Which store?"

"Foxborough. Um, I don't have a number or anything"

"That's fine."

Zach typed in something, the keys clacking over the phone line. "Alright," he said. "So they don't have a general manager right now. They're being run in the interim by Gary McDonald. Is that what you needed?"

"What about before that?" James asked. "Who was the manager before?"

Another moment of typing. "Phyllis Danforth," Zach said.

James wrote her name down. "Do you know what happened to her?"

"It says here she was laid off during a round of staff cuts," Zach said. "I don't have any information beyond that."

James had a bad feeling forming in his stomach that he was right about this hunch. "Thanks," he said. "I think that's what I needed."

"Well, let me know if you need anything else. Anything I can do to help, seriously."

"I'll keep that in mind," James said.

He hung up a second later and immediately went to his computer. He typed Phyllis Danforth's name into the search bar and his heart sank as an obituary showed up as the first result. A quick scan showed that it was the correct Phyllis Danforth, who had been laid off in the first week of November. Of course, this wasn't mentioned in the obituary, but he could put it together himself. He scrolled back to the search engine and through the results. Sure enough, a fundraiser page for her family was the fourth result.

Loving mother, full of life and compassion, loved her job. Lost her battle with depression after losing her job. All proceeds from the fundraiser going to her children and grandchildren.

James let out a long breath. He needed to take a shower, then he needed to call Father McEnerney. But he had a feeling this case was coming to a close, and no one was going to feel good about it in the end.

Chapter 21

Maybe the anointing was overkill, but James would take it if it meant not driving off the road and nearly dying again. If the worst he got was a little acne from the oils, then so be it. He nodded solemnly as Father McEnerney swiped his forehead with oil, saying something too quiet for James to hear. He wished he could offer the same protection to the priest, but he apparently had set himself up, so he didn't seem concerned.

They were sitting in James's car outside of Polly Grace's house again. He'd filled Father McEnerney in on their last visit, and he wasn't sure what they were going to accomplish here. But the Father had insisted he wanted to see it.

"Should we have brought a medium in?" James asked as Father McEnerney tucked his small black bag into the back seat of the car.

"Oh, probably," Father McEnerney said. "But they weren't going to spare one of that team right now."

"Is the entire security team in Ashburnham?" James asked.

"Not the whole thing? They don't tell me everything, but as far as I know, it seems to be about half of the Foundation's total agents protecting that house right now."

A mix of frustration and relief surged through James at that. On one hand, he was relieved that those children were protected. But on the other hand, there were so many other things that needed attention. He knew cases hadn't stopped. The hose was just blocked up to a slow trickle until they finished this one. Because the Delinskys had money and the Foundation wanted some of that money to keep flowing their way.

Apparently his feelings on the matter were obvious, because Father McEner-ney shrugged as he adjusted his Roman collar. "What are you going to do, argue with the higher-ups?" he asked. "Not like it's worked in the past."

"Let's just get this done so that we can go back to helping people who aren't multimillionaires," James muttered.

They got out of the car and walked into the rundown yard of the tiny cottage. Most of the snow from the other day had melted, exposing shriveled plants and waterlogged lawn decorations. James recognized a small scarecrow from the dollar store as it lay beside the worn pathway. The idea of this powerful conjurer going to Dollar Tree was just too weird to comprehend, so instead of trying to decipher his feelings on the matter, he just kept walking. James kept his eyes on the window, but the tattered curtain stayed in place as they made their way up the tiny walkway and to the front door.

Father McEnerney knocked on the door. Just like James had the other day, he paused and waited, but nothing came. He tried again. Still nothing.

"Hang on," he said, stepping off the stairs.

James watched as he walked toward the side of the house, stepping over a broken lawn chair that was half-covered in dirty snow. He had his hands plunged into the pockets of his long, black coat as he casually disappeared around the corner.

James followed in time to see Father McEnerney looking in the side windows. "What are you doing?" James hissed.

"I'm trying to see if she's here," Father McEnerney replied evenly. "She knows we know. It's not like we have secrets now."

He looked inside again as James stood at the corner of the house, glancing around wildly for any sign of somebody spotting them. If someone caught them casing some old lady's house, there was going to be hell to pay, priest or not.

"Nobody in the kitchen," Father McEnerney muttered. "Alright, let me check out back."

He walked to the back of the house as James followed, swearing under his breath. There was nobody in the back, not in the tiny mudroom or in what

Father McEnerney said had to be the bedroom.

"Great, then let's go before someone calls the cops," James said.

"She's not here," Father McEnerney said as they walked back to the car.

"Maybe she's just getting groceries," James suggested.

From the priest's skeptical look, he knew he wasn't convincing either of them. But if she wasn't there, where was she? And what was she capable of doing next?

* * *

James dropped Father McEnerney off at the Cottage at Delinsky Cove, sparing a disgusted look for the mansion before driving back to Leominster. It was a dull gray outside and even the trees along the highway seemed muted, like they'd been drained of life.

He was exhausted. And angry. And this case might be the turning point. The Foundation had never been a charity, he knew that. But the glaring difference between how they handled most cases and how they were falling over themselves for this case was too much to ignore.

As soon as he got in the door at Headquarters, Amelia was waiting for him. "Oh no," was the first thing that escaped his mouth at the sight of her.

"We have a problem," she said.

"Of course we fucking do. What is it?"

"Zach Delinsky just called a minute ago. I tried to reach you through Father McEnerney, but he said you'd already dropped him off."

"We were at Polly Grace's house. She was gone."

"Yeah, we might know where she went."

James's stomach dropped. "What happened?"

"Zach is on his way to the Foxborough Delinsky's location. He said that they just got a panicked call from Gary, the interim manager, that there's something going on in the store. He said Gary didn't say what, just that there was something evil, and he wasn't staying. So Zach's father sent him to check."

"I'll go," James said, fishing his car keys out of his pocket.

"Hang on, I'll come too."

James held up a hand to stop her. "Amelia," he said. "That's probably not a good idea."

There was a flash of anger across her face, then it drained away as she sighed. "You're right," she said. "I'll slow you down."

"No, I'm nervous you might get hurt again. Jesus. Look, can you stay on comms with me? I don't have my phone, so I'm going to be relying on the comm system and I'm going to need you. Who's here?"

"Gabriella and Madelyn."

"I'm going to take Gabriella with me. We'll go see what's going on. Maybe it'll end up being a simple cleanse or something."

They both knew that wasn't true, but neither of them was about to say it. Instead, James called up the stairs, "Gabriella!"

A second later, she poked her head out of the kitchen, long, blonde hair tied up in a messy knot as she ate an apple. "Yeah?"

"I need you to go to Foxborough with me."

She clearly knew what had happened, because she didn't say anything. Instead, she headed for the supply closet.

"What do we need?" she asked.

"All the standard stuff," James said. "Holy water, knives. Hell, toss the cryptid supplies in there. I think she's still human."

"And who are we going after, again?"

"I think whatever is happening at Delinsky's is linked with that Polly Grace woman we haven't been able to find," James said. "If she's there right now..."

Zach was on his way there right now, James realized with a force that stopped him cold. Shit, he could be walking right into a trap. Even if he wasn't a monster, he was a Delinsky, and that made him just as much a target as the others.

James ran into his office, ignoring Gabriella's call after him. His desk was a mess, and it took a few panicked seconds of tossing papers aside and onto the floor before he found Zach's business card half-crushed beneath a stained

Tupperware lid. He grabbed it and, with shaking hands, dialed Zach's number.

Zach picked up after a couple of rings. "James?"

"Zach, don't go into the store," James said. "It might be a trap."

"What do you mean?"

"I mean, they're the ones who did it. There's two staffers at the Foxborough store. They hired someone to kill your family and you might be driving right into their trap right now."

James heard Zach's brakes screech as the other man's car stopped short. "Tell me you're not on the highway," James said.

The car started up again. "I'm almost off it," Zach said. "Hang on, I'm going to pull over as soon as I'm off the exit."

It was quiet for a moment and James expected to hear steel colliding with steel, that screeching, screaming sound that still haunted his dreams after hearing it too many times in real life. But there was nothing, and he almost didn't believe it when he heard Zach speak again. "Tell me everything."

His voice was clipped and almost calm, but James could tell it was a front. It was almost identical to the way Bradley acted when shit was falling apart on a case. He took a deep breath. "I don't have any definite facts," he admitted. "But we met two staffers there before me and Amelia were in that accident, and they all but admitted they hired someone to curse your family. It's revenge. Their manager was fired, and she killed herself."

"Fuck."

Zach's voice was so quiet that James almost didn't hear him over the sound of cars driving by. "We're on our way, but it's going to take at least an hour," James continued. "Don't go into that store."

"But my father-"

"I don't care what your father said to do," James snapped. "Zach, listen to me. If you go in that store, you will die. Do you understand? This is personal. Stay out of there, for Christ's sake."

"What should I do?"

James's heart sank as he realized he didn't have a good answer to give. "Where are you?" he asked.

"I'm just off the highway in Milford," Zach said.

"Don't keep driving," James ordered. "Stay in your car. Don't talk to anyone, don't let anyone in. For the love of God, do not go to that fucking store."

"I can't not-"

"DON'T!" James roared. "Goddammit, if you love your nieces and nephews at all, don't go near that place. You will die and they will have to deal with it."

There was silence on the other end. James knew Zach wasn't used to being told no, no millionaires were. But then there was a reluctant sigh. "You're right," Zach said, voice watery.

"Of course I am," James said, trying to keep his tone light. "I'm an expert. Hey, it's going to be okay."

"Yeah."

"James, I'm ready."

Gabriella's voice came into his office, and he looked up and nodded at her. "Listen, we're leaving now," he continued. "This isn't yours to fix. We're going to take care of it."

"Thank you."

"I mean it, though. Do not leave your car. Go sit in a parking lot until you hear from the Foundation. Turn it off. Do a fucking crossword while you wait."

Zach gave a tearful laugh and James was satisfied that he was telling the truth when he said he'd stay. "Call this number if you need anything and they'll pass your message onto me."

"Just be careful," Zach said.

"I will," James promised. "You too. Just stay safe, it'll be over soon."

Chapter 22

James hung up and hurried out to where Gabriella was waiting. "I caught him in time," James said as they went down the stairs. "He's not going to go into the building. I made him promise not to even turn on his damn car again until I tell him to."

"So, what's our plan?"

"We cleanse that store. Go in, see what's there. If it's physical, we tranq it and get it out of there. If it's not, we seal off the store, cleanse it, and keep working the case. Maybe try to get Janis and Jeremy to stop this, if they are there. I'm going to hope this is the end of it, because I'm fucking sick of this."

The wind was bitterly cold as they walked to his car. The neighbors across the street had an elaborate Christmas display up that he hadn't noticed as he'd walked in earlier. Santa and his reindeer were blinking on the roof while the yard had a gaudy nativity scene with what he was pretty sure were Peanuts characters. But before he could look too closely, they were in the car and heading down the road.

"We need to get it out of the store," James said. "And protect whoever's in there. My guess is that these two jerkoffs got too confident with their relationship with this Polly Grace nightmare. If she's destroying their shop, maybe she's not on their side at the moment."

"What, do you think the Delinskys paid her more?"

"Please, this is too undignified for them," James said, pulling onto the main road. "No, they kill people by preventing them from collecting unemployment. Totally different."

"You hate them, don't you?"

James sighed. "Don't you?"

"I guess, yeah. But you seem like you get along with Zach. Even all my comments aside, which I still stand by."

"I do," James said. "Yeah, I like him. He seems like a good guy, if a bit of a rich kid. But his family is revolting. And the more I learn about them, the more I hate them. I hope this makes him think about his future in the company."

They were quiet for a moment as James pulled onto Route Two. It was almost fully dark now, and the traffic was pretty light on this side of the highway, though he could see the river of headlights on the westbound lane. "Listen," he said. "This could get ugly."

"I know," Gabriella said.

"Like, violent. This thing already tried to kill me and Amelia."

"What, like nothing's ever tried to kill me on this job?"

She wasn't wrong. "Still," James said. "Just be careful, okay? We don't know exactly what we're walking into and we're definitely not prepared enough."

Gabriella didn't answer, but he wasn't too worried about it. Instead, he focused on driving, trying to keep his mind occupied by looking for his next exit and not on exactly what they were driving into. After a little while, Gabriella spoke without looking at him.

"Do you think they'll just keep sending us into cases like this?"

"Like what?"

"Like, unprepared and hoping for the best?"

"Of course."

Another beat. "Do you think if Robin had succeeded, that would still be the case?"

This time, it wasn't a curse that made James nearly drive off the road. He veered the car back into the lane and tried to keep looking at the highway ahead of them. "Are you kidding me?" he asked. "Gabs?"

"No, seriously. I'm not looking for pity, I'm asking the question. Do you think if he'd killed me, he would have gotten the support he was trying to get?"

"I don't know. Dammit, why are we even talking about this?"

His hands were shaking on the steering wheel. "I don't know," he snapped. "But we're not going down that road. We're never going down that fucking road. He was wrong."

His voice was rising by the end of it, and he stopped short to avoid shouting at her. The last thing they needed was to be fighting and scattered when they got to the actual fight in thirty minutes.

"They're wrong," he said finally, keeping his voice low as Gabriella looked over at him. "The Foundation is wrong to under support us. The Delinskys are wrong for how they treat their employees like they're nothing, and these two are wrong for murdering people. It's that simple and not at all simple, you know? So let's just finish this so we can get back to doing work that's actually fulfilling."

Gabriella didn't answer and James was afraid to look over in case he'd made her cry. But then he stole a glimpse and saw her looking thoughtfully out the windshield ahead of them.

"Okay," she said. "But do you think if we solve this, then maybe either of the extremely wealthy parties involved in this mess will pay us a little extra for our trouble?"

"Not a chance in hell."

Chapter 23

James was trying to hide the nerves bubbling in his stomach as they pulled into the parking lot outside of Delinsky's, but he knew he was doing a piss-poor job of it. As he looked over at Gabriella getting her supplies set up in the passenger seat, he could tell she was nervous too. "You good?" he asked.

She looked up, holding an amulet in a slightly shaky hand. "Yeah, I'm fine."

"As soon as I know what we're dealing with, we act, but not before. I need you to stand back, okay?"

"James-"

"I'm not saying to leave," he continued. "I'm saying let me see if this thing is human. Polly Grace might physically be here, but probably not. But if Janis and Jeremy are here and they're fucking around with her power, we might be able to stop them and end this now. I'm going to need you to have my back."

"Got it."

"Are you protected?"

It comforted him to see the size of the blade she was strapping around her waist as he asked. "Yeah," she said. "All blessed, all purified. I've got holy water, a blade, amulets. Tinctures. I could go for some armor, but I guess I'll have to ask for that for Christmas."

"You and me both."

James had the tranquilizer gun holstered on one hip and a taser on the other. He felt a little ridiculous with his cryptid kit on, but it seemed like the best option when he wasn't sure what he was going into right now. That, plus salt, an iron blade, and the same herbal tincture, should cover most of the situations they might find in there.

And if it didn't, then they were just in their usual supremely under-prepared state.

He hooked the camera onto his chest and turned it on. "Amelia, you there?"

"Got you," Amelia's voice came over the comms.

"Do you have visuals?"

"Yeah, I can see Gabriella. Nice knife."

Gabriella laughed, her hand moving to the knife on her hip. "It's my new favorite."

"It's a good look. Alright, I'll stay quiet unless you talk to me first."

"Confirmed," James said.

He turned to Gabriella. "Ready?"

"Yeah, ready."

They were parked at the far end of the parking lot, which was still chaotic with holiday shoppers despite whatever was going on inside Delinsky's. James got out of the car and Gabriella followed. The weight of his kit was comforting, though he was also feeling a little exposed going in through the front door like this.

They walked silently through the parking lot, ignoring the stares of people walking by. James expected the doors to Delinsky's to be locked, but they opened with a single tug and he walked straight in.

The Christmas music was still pumping through the speakers, this time "Silent Night" playing at a volume that hurt his ears. But the lights were out, only the dim emergency lamps glinting off the golden decor to provide any light as they walked into the shop. The shadowy clothing racks loomed over them and every hair on James's body stood on end as he walked, knife in hand, as his eyes darted all over the room.

A figure raced out of the shadows ahead of him and he had his knife raised before he realized it was Janis. She was sobbing hysterically as she ran toward him. In the darkness behind her, he could see massive, misshapen racks of clothing, but no other people. At least not yet.

"She's here, she's here," Janis cried as she hurried over.

Was this a trap? Not that it mattered, because she was already right in front of him. But before she could get close enough to touch him, James had his knife at her throat. "Tell me what's going on," he demanded. "What did you fucking do?"

She was crying almost too hard to speak, but then the words tumbled out in a nearly incoherent mess. "We needed to get back at them," Janis sobbed. "They were - they hurt us. And Phyllis was so sad. They used her so much and then just fired her right before the holidays. She killed herself, and it was their fault. And they needed to pay for what they did. It was worth the cost, and they needed to FUCKING PAY!"

She screamed the last two words, and James jumped, but didn't drop the knife. He had a feeling they were being watched from the darkness, eyes blazing into the back of his neck. As far as he could tell, Amelia was still muted on the line, also watching everything. Her presence gave him a little comfort.

"Where's Jeremy?" he asked as, out of the corner of his eye, he saw Gabriella shift to watch his back.

"Dead," Janis sobbed.

That's when James realized why the shelf behind the dress rack looked so misshapen. It had been too dark to see clearly, but his eyes were now adjusted to the dim light of the store.

James's stomach fell as he saw Jeremy's body hanging above her. His feet were latched onto the rack, while his arms were strapped to the wall display behind him with two overpriced belts. Blood poured from his open mouth as his eyes stared blankly ahead.

"Jesus Christ..." James muttered, taking a step back.

"We told her we'd pay her, we had the money, it was just going to take a little while," Janis continued as though he hadn't just noticed the grisly scene behind her. "We asked for just a little more time, but she told us it had to be now. And when he tried to fight her-"

She cut off with a small hiccup. "Gary left."

"The only smart person here," James said. "What were you thinking?"

"We needed to make them pay for what they did!" Janis said. "They needed to know that they messed up when they hurt Phyllis, and they needed to hurt for it too. I've worked here for four years and I've never gotten a raise. Jeremy was here for ten. Phyllis gave them twenty fucking years, and they killed her for it. They need to hurt and they need to die."

"Do you have any idea what you've done?" Gabriella demanded from behind James as the music cut out so abruptly that his ears rang in its absence. "Where did she go?"

"I don't know!" Janis exclaimed. "I don't know if she was really here! She killed Jeremy, and she disappeared, but I don't think she's gone. And I can't pay her. You need to help me!"

An astral projecting murderer. Fantastic. "We'll do our best," James said. "But you need to tell me everything. You hired someone to kill the Delinskys for you. Polly Grace?"

Janis nodded rapidly, and James tried to focus on her instead of the corpse behind her. "I wanted to do something else, but Jeremy convinced me and he was right. She killed the owners, and they all panicked. The ones who made the choices died and the ones who benefited from it got to feel what it's like to be scared, to not be in control."

Something clattered to the ground in a far corner of the store. James felt Gabriella jump behind him and tried to stay focused. Janis's face went even paler in the dim light.

"We were behind on the payment, just by a couple of days. She told us the consequences would be- would be severe, but I didn't think it would be this bad. I can't afford to pay her right now."

"James!"

James whirled around in time to see Gabriella lifted off her feet and tossed backward down the aisle. She got up immediately, blade in hand.

"Who are you?" she demanded, spinning around as a formless shape moved behind her in the darkness, fluttering at the edges like smoke. Just like Rita Delinsky had described.

James had his holy water in hand, feeling useless as he pulled one of his amulets off his neck and tossed it toward Janis. "Put it on!" he barked.

She put it over her head with a shaking hand. "What do I do?"

"Stay right the fuck there. Don't move."

Something collided with him, knocking the wind out of him. It felt almost human, but the power behind it was too fast to be normal. "Got out of here!" he snapped toward it.

Another icy tendril of wind. No, it wasn't human, no matter how much force it had. This was magical. It was just energy, and he knew how to deal with energy. Maybe they could end this here.

James took a deep breath, trying to unlock the Latin that usually flowed naturally when he was doing a cleansing. That was all this was. This wasn't Polly Grace, this was her just her power, and he needed to clean it out.

He turned back to Janis, who was wide-eyed and angry under her terror. Then he started chanting, trying not to think too hard about the words as he tossed the holy water into the shadows. Jeremy's body still dangled in view and James's stomach turned as water splashed off the man's shoe. Gabriella was behind him, guarding his back as he performed the ritual he could do in his sleep. There were no candles, but the emergency lights gleamed off the gold fixtures in a way that looked like fire. Maybe if he mentally convinced himself they were flames, the ritual would work just as well. He needed to sanctify the space, just enough that a salt circle wouldn't seal Polly Grace's magic inside with them.

Still talking, the Latin words flowing meaninglessly past his own ears, he reached for the salt on his supply belt. If he could get Janis within the circle, maybe that and the amulet would keep her safe long enough to cleanse Polly Grace's influence from this shop.

It was fine, this was fine. He'd finish, they'd seal the doors, and then they'd get Janis safe and go after Polly Grace in person.

He was still thinking this when something yanked Janis up to the ceiling, screaming and thrashing against the force that was holding her there. James made eye contact with her for a split second from twenty feet below. And then she was falling. He ran to catch her, but she hit the stone floor of the shop with a sickening crunch and lay still.

Gabriella was directly behind him as he ran. Ritual forgotten, he reached Janis's crumpled body. It was okay, people survived heights like that. Madelyn had fallen from higher and she was over at Headquarters right now. It was fine, it was fine, it was–

Janis was dead. Empty eyes stared up at him from her broken face, which was tilted at an impossible angle on a snapped neck. But before he could even begin to react, there was a voice in his ear. Impossibly sweet, like syrup trickling into his brain.

"The debt is paid," the voice whispered.

And then the lights came back on.

Chapter 24

It took the Foundation too long to send agents to Foxborough to help James and Gabriella. After a few seconds of stunned silence, Amelia had broken onto the line, saying she was getting the Foundation on the phone now. Her voice had been flat and stunned, but James heard her talking to someone a few minutes later, and that was when it sank in that they were done.

James technically handed over the case to them at that moment, giving them all the information and asking Amelia to contact Zach and let him know things were over. Part of him felt like he should be the one to call Zach, but the idea of doing anything but looking down at Janis's body, which Gabriella had draped with a seven hundred dollar white dress, seemed impossible.

He left Jeremy's body where it was, not wanting to disrupt the scene too much before the Foundation got here with the police. He wished there was a dignified way to cover Jeremy as well, but anything he might try to drape over the man's body as he hung from the clothing rack would just look ridiculous.

They didn't deserve to look ridiculous.

As they waited for the few people who were left in Boston to make their way down the highway to Foxborough, the two of them stood guard over the bodies. Gabriella watched the entrance while James stayed where he was. This wasn't his first time dealing with death on the job. Not by a longshot. And he was pretty sure it wasn't Gabriella's either, even outside of their final encounter with Robin. But all he could think of was how much of a goddamn waste all of this was. So much death for nothing. The rich motherfuckers weren't going to learn the lesson that these two desperate, rage-fueled nobodies had died to teach them.

And what the hell were the two of them doing here alone? They could have been killed and apparently, the Foundation had security details for days. Bradley's comments about the Foundation cutting them further and further down echoed through James's head as he stood over the blank-eyed corpses while Gabriella guarded the door.

Someone came and tugged on the locked door handle, a Christmas customer with a frazzled look on her face. Gabriella shook her head grimly, and the woman flipped her the finger before storming off. Gabriella turned to see James watching.

"Whatever," she muttered.

Forty minutes later, the Foundation was on site, along with the local police. The two officers in charge of the scene looked scared in a way that was both satisfying and infuriating to James. He stood aside with the agent who was actually in charge and gave him all the details of what had happened.

"What a fucking waste," the agent, a fifty-something man with a stout frame and a long beard, said, shaking his head as the bodies were wheeled out the front door.

"They made a deal with a conjurer," James said. "I tried to keep her safe, I swear."

"I know, man," the agent said. "You did what you could, but you can't save people from themselves. Now we need to find this Polly Grace character. I'm surprised the Foundation didn't have this information already. Where did you say you heard about her?"

"A friend."

The man waited for another second, then nodded knowingly. "Alright, alright, I can respect an anonymous source. You did good today, Captain. I'm sure McGovern's going to want to talk to you when you get back to your headquarters, but I'm all set with you for now."

James nodded his thanks, then got Gabriella and walked out of the store. It had already been dark when they arrived, and now he had no idea what time it was. Late. But the mall was still open, despite the fire trucks and ambulances parked haphazardly outside of Delinsky's. The parking lot was crowded and people tossed curious looks at the door before walking along to the next entrance.

"Drop you at home?" James asked Gabriella.

"Are you going home after?"

"I wish," he said. "I need to meet with McGovern first. But come on, I'll bring you home. I know you're on in the morning."

She could argue that he was too, but she just nodded and followed him out across the lot. As they got into his car, a pickup truck stopped to let them out and claim his parking space.

"I don't feel good about this one," Gabriella said as they pulled onto the highway a few minutes later, after updating Madelyn on her cell phone.

"I know," James said.

"Do you feel any better about it?"

"No."

He didn't even want to think about it. Absolute fucking waste, everywhere he looked in this case. He wanted to go back, have his meeting with McGovern, write the final report, and never think about it again.

"What about Polly Grace? She got away."

"Obviously. It's not like we had a net we could catch her in."

James surprised himself with the harshness of his tone. Apparently, it was obvious to Gabriella as well, because she glanced at him in surprise. He shook his head.

"Sorry," he said. "I shouldn't talk to you like that. I didn't mean—we're not equipped to deal with her. Not right now. We need a whole lot more time to figure out what she's capable of, and we need more than holy water and Latin. But we'll figure it out."

"Sure."

They drove quietly the rest of the way back toward home. James got off the highway a few exits after he normally did and followed Gabriella's instructions to her apartment.

"Nice place," he said as they pulled up in front of a renovated boarding house with cheerful Christmas decorations on the front.

"Thanks," she said. "I really like it so far."

"You gonna be okay?"

She shrugged. "Of course. I'm going to go order Chinese food and take a hot shower. This is our job, right?"

"Right. Good night, Gabs."

He waited until she was safely on the other side of the front door before he began driving back toward Leominster. Madelyn and Graham were expecting him back soon, so he got on the highway and went straight there rather than meander the back roads with his thoughts like he wanted to. Any other time, McGovern could wait for him. He had to do enough waiting on the Foundation's behalf that maybe it was time they waited on him. But James wasn't about to do that to his team.

Chapter 25

When James got back to Headquarters a little while later, Madelyn was sitting in the living room. "Well, that's that solved," James said as he got to the top of the stairs.

"How are you doing?" Madelyn asked.

"Tired." He laughed slightly. "Are you on tonight?"

"Graham is, I'm not," Madelyn said. "Amelia's on her way back. She had to go over to Ashburnham to deal with the Delinskys. She sent Bradley home a little while ago, but I said I'd stay on comms til you got here."

"You can head out," he said. "I'm just going to have a quick meeting with McGovern, then I'm leaving too."

Madelyn slowly stood up, and the yellow lamplight caught the livid scar over her eye. He thought about the way Janis had fallen, her body picking up speed every second as it crashed toward the floor. It must have been terrifying.

Madelyn must have been so scared.

As though she could sense his thoughts, Madelyn looked at him. "None of us are happy with this case," she said. "We all see it. Don't worry."

James laughed. "At least I'm not alone."

"Absolutely not. Good night."

She started walking toward the door, her stride smoother than he'd seen it at all this week. As she left, James headed into his office. He didn't need to call McGovern just yet. He could sit on the couch for a second and catch his breath. Then he'd get up, have that stupid meeting, and then go home and get some sleep before starting it all over tomorrow.

He walked into his office and nearly jumped backward into the closed door as he realized, yet again, that the couch was already occupied.

Bradley was lying on the hideous floral couch, clearly asleep. He didn't move as James walked in. One arm dangled over the edge of the couch and on the floor next to him, James spotted a textbook with its soft cover half-crushed beneath its weight. A worn backpack sat next to it, its contents spilling onto the floor.

Trying to get his heart rate back under control, James stood over Bradley and shook his shoulder. "Hey," he whispered.

Bradley muttered something but didn't wake up. James tried again. "Hey, Brad, wake up, bud."

"He's your fucking cat," Bradley mumbled, then rolled over so that his back was facing James.

Whatever, he could stay there for a while. James needed to get this meeting over with.

He went to his desk and opened his email to find the meeting invitation from McGovern at the top of his inbox. It was marked for fifteen minutes ago. He opened it, and after a moment, McGovern's face was on the screen.

"James, there you are!"

"Here I am."

He could see himself in the small square at the corner of the screen. He looked half-dead, dark shadows under his eyes and hair sticking up from running his hands through it so many times on the drive home.

"Agent Forester has updated me on everything you two discussed at the scene. It's a shame things ended the way they did."

"Agreed," James said.

"The Delinsky family has been notified, of course. When this person, this conjurer, said the debt was paid, was she speaking to you directly?"

"It seemed like it," James said. "Her voice carried over the comms line where Amelia heard it too. I don't want to make assumptions, but it seemed like the death of the suspect fulfilled the terms of their agreement. Like, if she didn't get her pay, she'd take their lives instead."

"Did you find anything at the shop that might prove that? A contract or something?"

"No," James said. "Polly Grace has a home in Ashburnham, but we've been unable to contact her there."

"And the Foundation can't make a habit of just breaking into people's houses."

McGovern chuckled, the sound grating on James's frayed nerves. "No, I guess not," James said.

"No injuries this time, correct?"

Aside from the barely-adult who had given her life for an angry, worthless cause? "No," James replied. "No injuries to anyone on staff."

"Good," McGovern said. "Obviously medical care is important, but some of the higher-ups have been a little concerned about the costs in that department lately."

James's eyes flicked over to the couch, but clearly, Bradley hadn't heard his and Amelia's concerns come true just then. "We follow our safety protocols to the letter," he said, aware he was stepping into dangerous territory.

"Of course," McGovern said. "I don't doubt that. It's just money, that's all. Don't worry about it. Alright, how about you walk me through what happened?"

There were few things James would less rather do right now, but he launched into the story. He had just wrapped up when he saw Bradley sit up on the couch. The other man looked confused, then horrified as they made eye contact over the desk.

"I'll be right back," James said to McGovern, hitting the mute button.

He tilted the screen to make sure it wasn't showing anything beyond his desk, then walked over to where Bradley was scooping up his belongings. "Fuck," he was muttering. "Fuck, I'm sorry. I'm sorry. I know I shouldn't be in here."

"I don't give a shit that you're in here," James said. "I have no secrets, it's fine. Wait a few minutes for me to finish this meeting. I want to talk to you."

"No, I'm leaving. I shouldn't have-"

"Sit," James ordered. "Or I tell McGovern you're here and he invites you to this meeting with us."

Bradley looked over at the computer, then at James, and scowled. "Fine," he said. "What do you want me to do?"

"Just wait a sec, I think we're almost done," James said. "I don't know. Keep napping. Review the next chapter. Whatever. Just let me finish this real quick."

He went back over to the computer and sat down, unmuting the microphone again. "All set?" McGovern asked.

"Yeah," James said. "Sorry, a teammate had a question. Is there anything else? I need to get that report done."

"Yes, actually," McGovern said. "The Delinsky family wants to continue having the Foundation's protection. So we want your team to check in with them one or two times a week to help with any issues that might come up."

"You mean, like, check in with the agents there?" James asked.

"Oh, no, the agents will be leaving once we're certain they're safe. But the Delinskys have asked the Foundation to continue offering protection. Your team will take care of that as part of your coverage of North Worcester County."

James blinked for a second, sure he must have misheard this. "Okay," he said slowly, glancing over the computer at Bradley, who looked back at him with similar confusion. "So, how are we supposed to handle the extra workload? Will we be getting more staff?"

"James," McGovern chided. "You know how tight things are. You just got a new staff member a couple months ago."

"But you're asking us to add private security detail to our existing work," James said, still hoping maybe he'd missed something. "How are we going to do that with the current workload?"

"I have faith in you," McGovern said cheerfully. "If you send a rep over to their house on Monday, you can get it over with as the first thing in the week."

"Unless they need help with something."

"Of course."

"And then, what? Does that take precedence over any cases the Foundation sends?"

"No, we still need you to do your usual job."

Bradley went to stand, but James waved him off. "Due respect, sir," he said. "We barely have the resources to do what's expected of us now."

"We talked about this," McGovern said, a hint of frustration in his voice. "Things are tight right now. We'll offer whatever support we can, but I can't promise you resources that I don't have."

"Are the Delinskys hiring the Foundation on retainer for this work?"

"James, you know I'm not privy to the financial dealings of the Foundation. I can only give you the information I have."

Yeah, but James was perfectly capable of putting two and two together. "Listen," he said. "I've got staffers working doubles multiple times a week just to keep this place staffed. We still don't have a vehicle and I know that Bradley's sent in gas reimbursement requests multiple times for everyone who's had to use their own cars, myself included. I get it, all the branches have to deal with these kinds of things. But you're asking my team to become private security for a multi-million-dollar corporation on top of our already constant work schedule. I'm sorry, but no."

"Captain, this wasn't an invitation."

The use of his title sent an unpleasant shiver down James's spine and, glancing over at Bradley again, he could tell he wasn't the only one. "I know," James said. "But I've tried to be patient, I really have. This is too much, though. We'll continue to do our work to the highest standard possible, but I'm not sending anyone to investigate every little noise that happens at the Cottage. I need them here."

McGovern gave him a long look through the camera, and James kept his shaking hands out of sight. Then McGovern sighed.

"We can discuss it further later," he said. "But I'll bring your concerns up with my supervisors and see what I can do."

"Thank you," James said, meaning it.

They logged off the call a few minutes later, McGovern still chilly with him as he said farewell. James shut down his computer and rubbed a hand over his face. "Jesus Christ," he muttered.

Then he looked up to where Bradley was still eyeing him cautiously. "Hey,"

James said.

"I'm leaving."

James stood up and hurried over. "No, no, wait."

"What? I'm sorry, I shouldn't have come in here."

"I don't care. Man, you're like the third person I've found asleep on that couch this week. It's no big deal. Come on, sit back down."

Looking like he'd rather be anywhere else in the world, Bradley sat down on the couch. James considered bringing a chair over, then decided if he was already making things weird, he might as well sit on the couch for this, too.

"What's going on?" James asked, sitting down next to him.

"Nothing," Bradley said immediately. "I'm fine."

James regularly wanted to smack Bradley, so the feeling wasn't strange to him. But he also remembered that night over the summer when he'd reached his own breaking point and Bradley had been the one to pull him back from the edge. So instead, he sighed and took the plunge.

"Is it finals?" he asked.

Bradley froze. "No," he snapped.

Then he let his head drop back against the couch. "Yeah. How long have you known?"

"Not as long as I should have, considering I live with a former college professor and I keep finding textbooks around. Are you doing school full time while you're working here?"

Bradley nodded. "Yeah," he said again. "I have two classes on Thursdays and do three online."

"Jesus Christ. Why didn't you tell me?"

"Because it's none of your business?"

James bit back any reply he could give to that. Instead, he just gave Bradley an even look. After a moment, Bradley finally looked him in the eye.

"It's fine," he insisted. "I'm just having trouble with one of these classes and can't afford to fail the final. It's no big deal."

"Anything I can help with?"

"Not unless you're a biology tutor."

"I'm not," James admitted. "But look, you can use my office to study or whatever you were doing. What were you doing?"

"Studying," Bradley said. "I can't focus on my apartment, it's too loud. But I lost track of time and fell asleep. It won't happen again."

"I truly don't care if it does," James said. "When's your final?"

"Thursday."

"Okay, that's three days from now. Listen, how about you take Wednesday off to prepare? I'll cover your shift, it's no big deal-"

"No," Bradley interrupted. "No, it's fine. I'm fine, really."

He didn't look fine. He had that same look James recognized from his college roommate's face during midterms, just before he'd snapped and locked James out of their room. But James also knew he wasn't going to win this one.

"If you're sure," he said.

"I am. I'll get going. Really, I'm-"

"Don't apologize again. It's weird."

Bradley glared at him, but it was halfhearted. But instead of arguing, he just looked at James. "You look like shit."

James laughed. "Yeah, you're one to fucking talk."

Bradley huffed a laugh and James yawned widely, covering his mouth. "Go home," he said. "Go get some rest."

"Are you leaving too?"

He was about to say no. That he wanted to finish the report and wrap this case up forever. But judging from the expectations that McGovern and the Delinskys had, and the fact that Polly Grace had vanished, it was far from over.

"Hell yeah," he said instead, standing up. "I'm going to bed."

Chapter 26

"Chris has another roommate interview lined up for us."

James looked up from his computer at Graham, who was standing in the office doorway, a steaming mug of coffee in his hand. "Oh, yeah?"

"Yeah. The buddy of a buddy."

"Sounds like a treat."

Graham stepped into the room and sat down on the couch. "Should we bother?"

James shrugged. "I mean, I haven't had a chance to find anyone. But after the last guy, the idea of living with anyone Chris suggests is losing its shine."

"I've been asking around a little," Graham said.

"Oh yeah? When have you had time?" James paused for a second. "Wait, have you been asking the team?"

Graham shook his head. "No. Well, I mentioned it to Bradley, but that's it."

"If he wants to live with his captain and his Psych 101 professor? Oh, I'm sure he jumped at the chance. He barely tolerates working with me."

"Of course he refused," Graham said with a laugh. "But it wasn't because of you, at least he didn't say it was. Something about keeping work and home separate."

James had nothing to say to that. He reached for his own coffee while Graham continued.

"Either way, though," Graham said. "We need to figure out a plan. Sorry for not discussing this with you in advance, but there's an apartment coming up for rent in two months. I just saw it this morning. Two bedrooms and way cheaper than our place now. I didn't know how long it would stay on the market, so I made an appointment to look at it tomorrow. Do you want to go with me?"

Moving would be a pain in the ass. He'd have to clean, he'd have to pack, and then they'd have to figure out first, last, and security. Maybe this was a bad idea. They could just take this new guy and stay put.

"Look," Graham said, interrupting James's anxiety spiral as it began. "It's work, I know. But it'd be cheaper, even with just us. And it looks like a decent place. Here, may I?"

Without waiting for an answer, he came behind the desk and leaned around James to start typing. "What if I was doing something confidential back here?" James demanded.

"Then it would be the first time in your entire life," Graham retorted, pulling up the apartment listing. "Here, check it out."

James had to admit, it was a nice place. It was definitely an older building that had been renovated into apartments, but the rooms were sunny and looked bigger than their current ones. He scrolled through to see a small kitchen, then a yard.

"Let's see where it is," he said, copying the address and pulling up a map.

It loaded a second later, and James realized why the street name had looked familiar. It was less than a block away from Headquarters.

"Oh, God," Graham muttered.

"Talk about home and work life," James said.

He clicked back to the listing. "It is a nice place."

"And no weird roommates," Graham said.

"Why? Where are you going?"

Graham just looked at him and shook his head. He clearly didn't give James the credit he deserved for being hilarious.

"Yeah," James said. "It's going to be hell to get it done, but this sounds good to me."

"So you want to go tomorrow? It's at noon."

He'd be here at work, but apparently, it was a three-minute walk away. "I'm in," he said.

He closed the browser and Graham went back to the couch to pick up his coffee. "There's a small case that just came through," he said. "Amelia took it since you were busy. But she's sending me and Madelyn to take some statements down at City Hall."

"Poltergeist?" James asked.

"Yeah."

"Check your email," he said as he went back into his own inbox. "I've got a whole report on that from a couple of weeks ago."

He sent Graham the report. "Good luck," he said. "Report back, I'll be trapped here under the paperwork."

Graham started to walk away just as James remembered what he'd wanted to say to him earlier. "Oh, Graham!"

Graham stopped and turned around. "I also sent you the cryptid specialization modules that the Foundation has," James said. "If they're not completely useless, please let me know so I can die from shock."

Graham grinned at him. "I'll be sure to do that."

* * *

James got the last of the Delinsky paperwork sent off right before lunch. Even seeing their name on the top of his document pissed him off right now. The fucking audacity to expect him and the team to become their, what, their paranormal protection squad? And for McGovern to just throw that on top of their existing work as though it was no big deal. Unbelievable.

He knew exactly how it would go, too. There'd be a small thing, they'd investigate it, and be done. Then there'd be another. And another, though maybe not quite so paranormal this time. And eventually, they'd end up working exclusively for the Delinskys as their usual work turned into a side hustle.

No, even if McGovern thought it could work, James knew for a fact that it never would.

James walked out of his office and headed toward the kitchen. He'd packed lunch today, and for once, he was actually going to eat it. Sure, it was leftover pizza, but he wasn't buying new takeout today, so he'd count it.

Amelia was sitting in the living room, eating a sandwich and reading something on her phone. She looked up as he came in.

"Hey," she said. "I actually need to talk to you."

This was it. He knew without a doubt at that moment. She was leaving. It was a good thing for her. Hillsborough was a good branch, they knew their shit. She could run her team and maybe sometimes they'd still work together.

"Yeah?" he said, trying to keep these thoughts out of his tone. "What's up?"

"So I talked to the captain over at Hillsborough this morning."

"You're taking the job?"

"No, I turned it down."

The knot in James's stomach vanished just as he was trying to force himself to casually eat the pepperoni slice in his hand. He looked over at Amelia, hoping he hadn't misheard. "What?"

"Yeah," she said, scratching her head. "Listen, I appreciate you putting my name in for it. And someday, yeah, it'd be cool to be in charge. But I'm actually really enjoying being second in command for now. So I'd rather stay here with you guys."

"Are you sure?" James asked. "I don't want you to feel obligated to stay if you'd rather..."

"I'm sure," she said. "There will be others. I'm only twenty-five, I've got plenty of time."

He knew the relief was clear on his face by the way her expression softened. But rather than teasing him like he expected, she just smiled and stole a pepperoni.

Chapter 27

James was still irritated that the Foundation wouldn't pay for his new cell phone, but at least he had one again. Between an early upgrade and a rebate, he'd been able to get a decent enough price on it. And with his rent going down once he and Graham moved into the new apartment, it wasn't going to hit his budget too hard. But regardless, he rolled his eyes as he scanned the rejected reimbursement submission, then deleted the email.

His new phone rang, and he glanced over at it. The number was blocked. So it could be anyone from a sales call to Polly Grace, who still hadn't been found. He reluctantly picked it up.

"Hello?"

"Hey, James?"

The voice was familiar. "Yes?"

"Hi. It's Zach Delinsky."

Part of him wanted to hang up immediately, part of him wanted to stay on the line all day. "Hi, Zach."

"Hi."

There was a moment of awkward silence. "Um, what can I do for you?" James finally asked.

"Oh, right. Um, I wanted to let you know that I quit the company."

James walked over and closed his office door, then sat down on the couch. "Oh, yeah?"

"Yeah," Zach said. "I couldn't be a part of that anymore. Even if I wasn't the one directly hurting our employees, I was still part of it. And after everything that happened, I need to get away from all of that.”

“Good for you,” James said. “What are you going to do next?”

Zach laughed, the sound light and musical. “Oh, I have no idea,” he said. “I’m getting away today. Going to go somewhere warm and escape the cold for a little while while I decide.”

James glanced out the window, where the clouds were hanging low over the dirty gray snow lining the road. “Have fun,” he said, trying not to sound bitter.

If it showed, Zach ignored it. “Thanks,” he said. “I’ll be doing a lot of thinking while I’m away. I’m so furious with my family, but I can’t leave them. Not when the kids...”

He trailed off, and James waited patiently for him to regroup. “I can’t leave the kids to grow up in that environment without a single adult who actually cares about them,” he said. “So I’m leaving the business, but I’m not cutting ties.”

He said it as though he was looking for James’s permission to do this. To stay with his awful family. “I mean, yeah, that’s a good thing to do for the kids,” James said.

“My cousin is still gone,” Zach said. “I’ve been in touch with him, but he’s cutting all ties now that I know he’s safe. I don’t know if it’s guilt, fear, who knows? But he’s gone now.”

James remembered the other man and his fear during that first meeting. He couldn’t say he was surprised by this news.

“My flight’s boarding,” Zach said. “I have to go. This has been terrible, but I’m really glad I met you.”

Shit, was Gabriella right? “I’m glad I met you too,” James said, and he meant it.

The call disconnected, and James set down his phone. Vacation. Maybe he should take his right now. He could call Zach back, ask him where he was going and if he wanted some company on whatever tropical island he was headed to. Use some of those hundred vacation days and bend his no-dating rule for a little bit.

But then James thought about the rest of the Delinskys, and that plan evaporated as quickly as it had arrived. No, it would never work. It was a nice dream, but not nice enough that he could ever tolerate a continued connection with the rest of them. If he ever saw Zach again, it'd be a pleasant surprise. But no, he wasn't going there.

What he was going to do, however, was check his calendar and put in for a week's vacation right now.

* * *

James looked over at Amelia, who was staring in disbelief. Then he looked at Bradley, who was equally shocked. But he couldn't blame them, not when he felt just as surprised.

They were standing on the lawn outside of Headquarters, looking at the van that was currently parked in front of them. The replacement for the old van had arrived.

"This is..." Amelia shook her head. "This is the ugliest thing I've ever seen in my life."

"Did they solder two vans together to make this?" Bradley asked.

The van looked new, at least from within the past five years. And this should have been an improvement over the old van. But as James looked at it, he thought maybe Bradley was right. The back half, up through the sliding door, didn't seem to quite match the front half. Something about the shape of it was off. And the mustard yellow coloring seemed to change. But it ran, and it was theirs.

"Hey, did that... oh my God."

Gabriella's voice behind him made James turn around. She was wide-eyed as she stared at the atrocity in front of them. "This is it?" she asked.

"Apparently."

"Hang on, the others need to see this."

She darted back inside the house, leaving the other three out on the frozen grass. "Has it ever been inspected?" Amelia asked.

James opened the driver's side door and slid into the seat. It smelled fresh in here and the dashboard was free of dust. When he looked down, the carpets were freshly vacuumed. And when he turned the key in the ignition, it came smoothly to life.

"Well, RIP to the old one, I guess," he said.

Madelyn's laughter drifted over to them as she and Graham walked out of the house. "That is hideous!" she declared with obvious delight, limping slowly toward them.

Graham stood back a little to give her space, but the mingled horror and amusement on his face was apparent even from here.

"It's bigger," James said. "And there's cup holders in the back, look!"

He pressed the button to open the back door, but it stayed firmly shut. So instead, he hopped out of the van, went back, and opened it himself.

The two back rows were also freshly cleaned. As he climbed in, he noticed that the Foundation had replaced all the equipment that had been in the original van when it crashed. He could see a case of holy water and several blades he was pretty sure were actually the same ones he'd thought they lost.

"God, every monster in the county is going to see us coming," Amelia said.

James was climbing back out when the front door opened and Gabriella came out, holding a piece of paper. "We have a case!" she called. "City Hall is closed because something keeps locking people in the offices. They want us to keep it as quiet as possible and get over there immediately."

James looked at the hideous new van, then back at the team. This was the kind of case he wanted. Normal. Simple. Maybe he'd get to pick the lock to the mayor's office and heroically save him.

"Alright," James said. "Everyone get in the van."

END

Want a bonus epilogue?

Sign up for my email list over at BookFunnel and receive a FREE exclusive bonus epilogue to The Cottage at Delinsky Cove!

You'll also receive alerts for new books, sales, and exciting bonus content!

Sign up here: https://dl.bookfunnel.com/a9r8ux9tfi

Hillsborough County (North County Paranormal Unit #5)

Read on for a sample chapter of Hillsborough County: North County Paranormal Unit #5, now available from most retailers!

Hillsborough County: Chapter 1

The windows of the cozy fifties-style diner were fogged up against the cold night. Inside, the seats were worn in the narrow booths, with a bit of stuffing hanging out around the duct tape patches. The fries were fine while the burgers were amazing. And the place was packed with people, they'd barely gotten a seat. But it was the first time Gabriella had seen her boyfriend in nearly two weeks, so this greasy table was exactly where she wanted to be.

"-so I get to the house and not only is it completely deserted, but I don't think anybody's been there in months!"

Gabriella leaned in, fascinated, as Elliot took a sip of his drink, then continued his story. "So I call my dad and I'm like, 'Dad? Are we sure this is the right house?' And sure enough, it's actually the house in the next lot. Which is full of kids and really only needed a quick cleanup job. But Gabriella, if I'd been stuck at that first house, I don't think I would have made it tonight."

Originally, they had planned to go somewhere nicer and make a night of it. Then Elliot had needed to work an extra shift at his family's landscaping company and they hadn't been able to change their reservations at the original restaurant. He'd offered to reschedule with her, but between his work picking up at the end of the season, and the amount of cases Gabriella's team had been dealing with at the Foundation for Paranormal Studies, they had communicated almost strictly by text lately. So if their date involved wearing an oversized sweater and sitting in a cozy booth instead of a nice restaurant, Gabriella would take it.

"Where was the first house?" she asked, trying to push aside the itch of a new investigation outside of their deluge of cases.

Elliot waved a hand. "Still in Greenville, over off of Meadows Street. About a mile and a half from your mom's house."

She didn't know it, but she nodded along anyway. It had been several months since her mother had moved into her dream farmhouse over the border in Greenville, New Hampshire, but Gabriella still didn't know the area as well as she wanted to. Again, because she was still super busy with work all the time.

"So how about you?" Elliot asked. "How was work today?"

Gabriella shrugged. "Busy," she replied. "Nothing too exciting, but the flu is going around so we're short-staffed."

Elliot winced. "Christ, that's rough," he said. "But I guess historical restoration doesn't have to be too urgent, right?"

Gabriella agreed, that familiar little flare of guilt twisting in her stomach. Even after about four months together, she hadn't had the guts to tell Elliot her actual work involved hunting monsters and other paranormal phenomena. Sure, she mentioned occasional details in a "just-kidding" way to test the waters, but hadn't actually come out and told him these stories were true. He didn't believe in ghosts, she dealt with ghosts on a daily basis, and the idea of telling him just terrified her.

Elliot was fun and sweet. And normal. He was so amazingly normal. And when the rest of her life was spectacularly abnormal, getting out here with him was the exact escape she needed. It wasn't fair to either of them, she knew that, and she was going to tell him everything soon. But it didn't have to be today, right?

Or this year? Or ever?

"So, what are you working on?" he asked. "Anything exciting?"

Last night she'd dangled out a two-story window in order to banish a particularly angry spirit, relying only on what strength her teammates Bradley and Amelia had between them to keep her from falling to her death. "Nothing exciting," Gabriella said, taking a sip of tea with a smile. "Just... restoration. Old buildings, that kind of stuff."

The lies were coming a little too easily these days, and she knew it wasn't a good thing. "The one I'm working on now is haunted," she blurted out.

Elliot looked at her in amusement. "Oh?"

"Yeah," she said, the words tumbling over each other as she gave in to the impulse to keep telling the truth. "A lot of them are. This one has a former owner who died in an accident in the woods behind the house. His spirit is still lingering there, scaring people off the property."

Elliot laughed. "Sounds scary," he said.

"The spirit turns the lights on, even though there's no functioning electricity in the house. And throws the furniture around. Sometimes it gets stacked in impossible patterns before we get there."

"And you really think it's a ghost?" Elliot asked, the slightly patronizing tone deflating Gabriella's hopes instantly.

This was the most honest she'd been with him. Even when she mentioned searching for a creature in the caves of nearby Purgatory Chasm with the South County team, she hadn't mentioned the fact that it had one watery eye and could smell them in the dark. She'd just said it was an animal they'd run across on a team-building excursion. Elliot hadn't questioned why her historical restoration work had led her there, or why she worked so many overnight shifts, but maybe that was because he didn't know what historical restoration entailed. She wasn't too sure either, it had been her cousin and captain James's cover story and she just ran with it too.

Gabriella shrugged, feeling a little foolish despite the fact she was all too aware that ghosts were real. "I couldn't have stacked those chairs like that," she said. "I don't think any human could have."

"There has to be a rational explanation," Elliot said. "What did they look like?"

So much for that fantasy. Regretting bringing up the topic now, Gabriella pulled a pen out of her purse and turned the paper menu over. Underneath the kids' menu, she traced out the elaborate stacking pattern of the chairs the team had seen when they'd walked into the home that morning.

"It's from *Poltergeist*," Elliot said, flipping the paper to look at it from the correct angle. "Someone's messing with you. Have you not seen *Poltergeist*?"

"Of course I've seen *Poltergeist*," Gabriella snapped.

Obviously aware he'd pushed too far, Elliot's amusement faded. "It's probably just one of the owners having fun with you," he said. "Sorry, I'm not trying to be a dick."

"No, it's fine," Gabriella said.

An awkward silence settled over the table and she couldn't decide whether she was more frustrated with Elliot for his skepticism or herself for bringing it up. Or for bringing it up, then letting him talk her out of it.

Yeah, she was more mad at herself.

The sound of Gabriella's phone buzzing in her purse broke the tension. She was about to ignore it and try to start the conversation up again on a different topic, but Elliot nodded toward her phone. "You should get that."

"Yeah, right."

She picked up her phone and glanced at the screen.

JAMES

Amelia's sick now. Any chance you can come in tomorrow? Obv no pressure.

No pressure, but she also knew that meant James would end up working a triple. And it would probably be his third since coming back from his vacation last month, a vacation she suspected was primarily spent worrying about what was happening at headquarters. Luckily, she didn't have any plans beyond staying out late tonight and sleeping in tomorrow. But unlike James, Gabriella was paid hourly. And the overtime pay was appealing since rent was coming up quickly. So she could both help him and make some extra money.

GABRIELLA

No problem. What time?

She set her phone down on the table to wait for James's response. "I'm picking up a shift tomorrow," she said.

"Good," Elliot said, a little tentatively. "I'm working too."

The phone buzzed again and this time she was grateful for anything that would break this tension.

JAMES

8?

It was coming up on ten now and she was exhausted after working doubles the past couple of days. If she wanted to get enough sleep to get through whatever tomorrow's case might be, then she'd need to leave soon.

"We should plan an actual date," she said. "Maybe a night away. Or at least a day trip somewhere."

Elliot smiled at her, warm and real. "The second we both have a day off, I'm all yours," he said. "Maybe we can go somewhere near you, since you come up here so often."

Relieved, Gabriella tried to remember some places in the area she hadn't had to go to for work. If they were going to be anywhere near her house, those places were becoming more and more difficult to find.

* * *

Gabriella drove home about twenty minutes later, still a little raw over their conversation, but feeling better that the night hadn't ended on a bad note. This was on her anyway, wasn't it? She couldn't just keep dropping hints that she dealt with ghosts the way she had been doing. Yeah, she'd technically told him the truth. The place she'd been working at was extremely haunted. But she needed to tell him her role in everything, without crumbling at any pushback.

The roads were empty by now as she drove down the dark, wooded streets she was getting intimately familiar with these days. She left the radio off, enjoying both the quiet and the crisp night air coming through her slightly cracked window. The heat was high enough to keep her hands from freezing to the steering wheel, but the cut of chilled air kept her awake as she made her way past old barns and houses. Everything was set back in the woods, so far that right now all she could see was the twinkling of lights through windows.

She knew people were going about their lives behind those walls, but they were detached enough that she drove alone with her thoughts.

Tomorrow was going to be hard. Hell, the next month was at this rate. This flu was intense and, despite everyone getting the flu shot, it seemed to have arrived at headquarters. Madelyn had been the first on the team to fall, followed by Amelia tonight. They were roommates, so Gabriella wasn't too surprised. But missing two people from a staff of six was going to hurt. She could just hope that she, Graham, James, and Bradley could avoid getting sick long enough to keep their branch of the Foundation for Paranormal Studies running as smoothly as it ever did.

The Foundation was an old, respected institution that discreetly investigated unusual phenomena and took steps to contain or eliminate paranormal danger in the New England area. While they were headquartered in Boston, they had county-level teams who did most of the work in their regions. Gabriella had joined about nine months ago on James's invitation. Despite her horrible first month on the job, she loved the work. It was underpaid and dangerous, but more satisfying than anything she'd ever done before. If she could have both her job and Elliot, then she'd have everything she needed.

As Gabriella crossed into Massachusetts, she considered going straight to work and just sleeping there. After all, there were three bedrooms set up for that purpose and she had spare work clothes tucked into a dresser in one of them. James was on the night shift tonight and she was pretty sure he wasn't there alone, but not positive. If she went over now, she could just sleep in a halfway decent bed there and not worry about commuting in the morning.

Gabriella shook her head, blinking hard to get the ache out of her eyes. There was no point in doing that. Her apartment was less than twenty minutes away from headquarters and there was plenty of time for her to sleep and be ready for tomorrow. She needed to go home, get her mind off work for a little while, and get some rest.

Maybe she should take a hot bath. The tub in her studio apartment was tiny, but she could probably get it comfortable enough to be worth trying.

As she pulled up in front of her small apartment building just outside of downtown Fitchburg, Gabriella could see colorful string lights glowing in the windows of her unit. Just like every time she saw them from the parking lot, the tension in her body eased slightly. They looked pretty and festive, but she knew that underneath it all, she'd put them up to keep herself safe from monsters under the bed. As much as it might have seemed like the fear of a young child, it had happened to her after her first case. And that meant maybe it could happen again.

It wouldn't because the captain that had put the monster there last time was dead. But it never hurt to be prepared.

About the Author

Amanda McCormack is the author of *North County Paranormal Unit*, the *New Winslow* series, and the urban fantasy novella *The Problem with Magic*. She's a lifelong Massachusetts resident whose passion for the region provides the inspiration behind a lot of her work. She loves ghost stories, public transit, and buying more candles than she'll ever actually use.

Contact Amanda at amanda (at) enfieldarts.com

You can connect with me on:
- http://www.enfieldarts.com
- http://www.twitter.com/ghost_munch
- https://www.instagram.com/enfieldarts

Subscribe to my newsletter:
- https://dl.bookfunnel.com/urq8hp0j9n

Also by Amanda McCormack

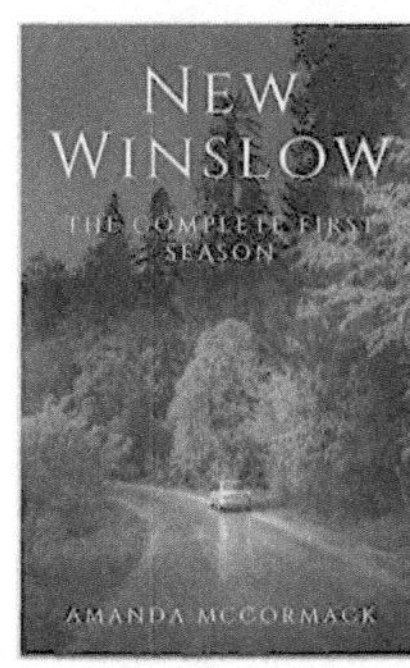

New Winslow: The Complete First Season
"You know, people don't exactly need a reason to stay in New Winslow."

A small town in the grip of a mysterious curse.

A population trying to live in its shadow.

And an impulsive promise that bring home two friends years after they left for good.

In New Winslow, stories weave in and out of each other. The town psychic seeks answers to something bigger than herself. Four friends warily reunite. And a man has made the most of his life, despite being trapped here for decades.

All that's been buried is slowly resurfacing. But will it change anything in a town that refuses to acknowledge its curse?

Hillsborough County: North County Paranormal Unit #5

An angry ghost

A relationship at risk

And a case that hits far too close to home

Gabriella has been uneasy about the ghost in her mother's new house since she first learned about its presence. Her mother insists Agatha is harmless, at least until an incident within the house convinces her to let the Foundation for Paranormal Studies investigate. Suddenly Gabriella, along with the rest of the North County branch, are consultants for another team with an ax to grind. And things only get worse for Gabriella when her boyfriend, a stubborn skeptic, finally learns the truth about her work.

With broken hearts among the living and dead, tensions between teams, and the flu ripping through North Worcester County, it's a bleak winter for Gabriella. Can she dig her way to the bottom of this case? Or will her failure cost her mother everything?

Hillsborough County is Book 5 in the North County Paranormal Unit Series!